A Thief at the Inn

Molly knocked on the Biddle sisters' door. "Gwen and I just wanted to borrow the coded message," she said when Ernestine stuck her head out. "We're going to work on it some more."

Ernestine stared at them. "But don't you have it already?"

Molly felt a sudden stab of alarm. "No. We left it in the strongbox, on your table," she said.

Ernestine stepped back and held the door open. Molly and Gwen peered in and saw that the coffee table had nothing on it.

"When we came back to our room, the box and the skeleton key were gone. We assumed you had them," Ernestine explained. "We also thought you were the ones who left the window open."

Molly pushed past Ernestine and hurried to the window. There was a tiny smear of mud on the sill. "Oh, no!" she gasped. It was suddenly, horribly clear what had happened.

The Biddles' suite had been burgled. And Sammy Slick's message had been stolen!

The Skeleton Key

WELCOME INN

#3 The Skeleton Key

by E. L. FLOOD

Rainbow Bridge®

Troll Associates

LIBRARY OF CONGRESS CATALOGING-IN-PUBLICATION DATA

Flood, E. L.
   The skeleton key / by E. L. Flood.
      p.   cm. — (Welcome Inn; #3)
   Summary: When three old women arrive at Welcome Inn bent on a strange mission, Molly and Gwen realize that they are about to experience another of their adventures.
   ISBN 0-8167-3429-1 (pbk.)
   [1. Buried treasure—Fiction.   2. Mystery and detective stories.]
I. Title.   II. Series: Flood, E. L.   Welcome Inn; #3.
PZ7.F6616Sk   1995
[Fic]—dc20   94-22762

Printed in the United States of America.

10 9 8 7 6 5 4 3 2 1

For Jenny and Charlie,
Who still love adventures,
And for Sam,
Who remembers those gangster days

CHAPTER ONE

"They look like witches," Gwen O'Brien announced. "Ugh! Creepy."

"Witches?" Molly, Gwen's sister, hurried over to the window of Welcome Inn's library. "Let me see." She stared at the three women who were climbing out of the battered station wagon that was Blackberry Island's off-season taxi fleet.

The old lady in front was tall and erect, with cropped iron-gray hair and a gaunt, hook-nosed face. Deep frown lines ran from her nose to the corners of her mouth. All Molly could see of her clothes was a pair of rubber boots sticking out from under a black rain poncho. Gwen was right. She could pass for a witch.

The woman right behind her was obviously

her twin. She had the same gaunt face and gray hair, but without the frown lines she looked like a kinder version of her sister. Her poncho was blue, and she wore a silky flowered scarf around her neck. Clutched in her hand was a red umbrella.

If the first two old ladies were witches, the third one must be a good fairy, Molly decided. Her face was plump, pretty, and rosy, and her silver hair looked as soft as a dove's wing. She wore white, high-heeled shoes and a white raincoat made of some kind of light, silky material.

The front door of the inn opened and Molly and Gwen saw their father, David O'Brien, go out on the porch to greet the guests. An instant later he was staggering under the weight of three enormous carpetbags. The first of the old ladies swooped past him, her black poncho billowing. The other two followed her inside, leaving Mr. O'Brien to juggle the bags as best he could.

"Hmm," Molly said thoughtfully. "They *could* be witches. Especially the one in black."

"I told you!" Gwen said.

Molly's brown eyes began to sparkle as her imagination got to work. "Wouldn't it be cool if they were witches? They could be here for some kind of ceremony. I read somewhere that witches do all sorts of weird ceremonies on the first day of spring. That's tomorrow. I wonder if I should call Josh?"

"Didn't he leave right after school yesterday?"

Gwen said.

"Oh, yeah." Molly suddenly felt deflated.

It wasn't fair. Here it was, spring break, and she had a week of freedom from school. A whole week to ramble around Blackberry Island in the soft, gray weather of late March. A whole week full of possible adventures! But with Josh Goldberg, who was just about her best friend, away on a ski trip until Wednesday, who was she going to have adventures *with*?

Of course, there was Gwen, but Gwen wasn't the ideal companion. You could count on her to come through in the end, but she complained a lot, and she always worried about getting in trouble.

Josh and Molly had gotten to be friends when he joined her and Gwen in their search for a pirate treasure, back when the O'Briens first moved to Blackberry Island. Molly hadn't trusted Josh right away, but he turned out to be a good friend. At first she didn't believe that the coolest kid in her class would want to spend time with a nobody like her, but after a while she'd come to see that his attitude was part of what made Josh so cool. He didn't worry about looking stupid. He just wanted to have adventures.

She had other friends now, but nobody else who felt the same way about adventures as she did. Ann Chiu was more interested in slumber parties and playing truth-or-dare. Molly liked that stuff, too, but sometimes it seemed kind of silly to her.

"Molly." Gwen's voice broke into her thoughts. "Do you think they really *are* witches?"

Turning back to the window, Molly caught sight of the departing taxi as it crept down the steep driveway. Witches didn't travel in taxis.

"No," she said. "They're just old ladies."

She heaved a sigh. Maybe it didn't matter that Josh would be gone for almost the whole vacation. It didn't look as if there was going to be much chance for an adventure this week, anyway. "Molly? Gwen?" their father called from the doorway.

"Dad, what's the matter with you?" Molly cried. His tall, thin frame was bent into a painful stoop.

"I think I threw my back out," Mr. O'Brien explained, trying to smile. "Whatever the Biddle sisters have in those suitcases of theirs, it weighs a ton. When I was carrying their things upstairs, I felt something go *crunch*."

"Oh, no!" Gwen exclaimed. Their father had always had back problems.

"I'll be all right," Mr. O'Brien assured them. "But I need to lie down. Could you two get the ladies their tea? They're unpacking now—they'll be down in twenty minutes."

Molly and Gwen helped their father into his study, nodding as he rattled off instructions about how to trim the crusts off the cucumber sandwiches in just the right way. "In fact, I'd better show you. Here, let me—ouch!"

"Dad, just calm down," Molly said as he clapped a hand to his back. "Don't worry. We know what we're doing. We'll take care of everything."

"Thanks," Mr. O'Brien said with a wan smile. "You won't have to chat with them too long."

"Chat?" Molly stared at her father in alarm.

"Well, sure," he answered. "But don't worry. Mom will be home from work soon, and then she'll take over." He lowered himself gingerly onto an old horsehair sofa and picked up the latest issue of *Coleoptera Journal*. He was an amateur bug scientist in his spare time.

"But—" Molly sputtered. "But what are we supposed to say?"

"Just small talk." He closed his eyes.

Retreating to the kitchen, Molly stared at Gwen in dismay. "I don't know how to make small talk with old ladies!"

Gwen shrugged. "We could ask how fast they fly on their broomsticks. I wonder if they could keep up with a jumbo jet?"

Sighing, Molly picked up a knife and started cutting the crusts off the bread for the cucumber sandwiches.

When the sandwiches were made, Gwen arranged some of Mr. O'Brien's homemade pastries on a plate while Molly measured loose tea and hot water into a large, flowered china teapot. Then the girls set everything out on a tray. Gwen held the door as Molly carried the tray into the front parlor, where the new guests were waiting.

The sister Molly thought of as the good fairy was perched on the love seat in front of the windows. "Tea! How nice," she trilled as Molly carefully set the tray down on the table.

Molly straightened and gave her a nervous smile. "May I pour you a cup, Mrs.—uh—" She broke off, aghast. She'd forgotten the name her father had mentioned.

"It's Biddle," one of the other two sisters called from the wing chair where she sat. Molly, glancing gratefully at her, recognized the nicer-looking of the twins. "She's Edith. I'm Ernestine. That's Ethel in the other chair. And we're all *Miss*, not *Mrs.*" She smiled at Molly. "Although Edith will tell you she was almost engaged once."

"Well, I was," the good fairy sniffed. "To the most wonderful man."

"He was a no-good—" Ernestine began.

"Girls! Don't start," the sister in black warned. She grasped the arms of her chair and stood up. "And who might you two be?"

Looking up at her, Molly gulped. Ethel Biddle was very tall. With her piercing dark gaze and beaked nose it wasn't hard to imagine her as a witch.

"I'm Molly, and that's my sister, Gwen," she said. "We live here."

14

"Goodness, Ethel, can't you tell?" Edith asked. "Look at that straight dark hair and those thin faces. The girls look just like that man who took our bags." Her eyes moved back to the tea tray again and her face brightened. "My, don't those tarts look tempting!"

"Our father made them," Gwen said proudly. "He's a gourmet cook."

"Is he?" Ethel didn't sound impressed. "Well, where's he got to? I want to talk to him about our rooms. Everything's been changed around!"

Molly hesitated, thinking it might be rude to tell the sisters how Mr. O'Brien had injured himself. Gwen, however, felt no such restraint.

"He threw his back out carrying your bags," she announced. "He's lying down."

"Oh, dear," Ernestine exclaimed. "It must have been Uncle Samuel's andirons! We should have warned him to take the bags one at a time."

Ethel snorted. "Fiddlesticks. Why, we carry them everywhere we go."

"Not anymore," Edith put in. "We haven't been able to afford a holiday for years."

"Edith, hush!" Ethel frowned. "We do not discuss the family finances in public."

Ernestine leaned forward in her chair and gazed at Molly. "They're solid metal, you see," she explained seriously.

Molly stared back, bewildered. "*What* are solid metal?"

15

"And what are andirons?" Gwen threw in.

Ethel stared at her. "Gracious," she said at last. "What are they teaching children in the schools these days?"

"Oh, dear," Ernestine said again. "These poor girls can't have any idea what we're talking about. Well, I suppose it is rather odd." Leaning forward, she picked up the teapot and poured tea into the cups. "Why don't you children sit down and have a pastry or two, and I'll see if I can't explain."

So it was that, much to Molly's surprise, she and Gwen found themselves crammed in next to Edith on the love seat, munching slices of apple tart.

"You see," Ernestine began, "our uncle was the late Samuel Biddle." She paused expectantly.

Gwen gave her a blank look. "Who?"

"Oh my!" Edith fluttered a hand in front of her face like a fan. "In this very house, dear Uncle has been forgotten!"

"Oh, hush," Ethel snapped. "Why should they know who he is? He died twenty years ago. They weren't even born yet!"

Molly tried not to jump as Gwen nudged her sharply in the ribs. "Weird," she whispered.

"Uncle Samuel was a philanthropist. He was rather well known in Chicago, our home town," Ernestine explained. "He moved to Blackberry Island when he retired in the 1950s. Right here to Welcome Inn, as a matter of fact."

"Here?" Molly was astonished.

Ernestine nodded. "In the very same suite of rooms where my sisters and I are staying now. We used to come here to visit him on our holidays."

"Of course, it wasn't Welcome Inn at the time," Edith put in. "It was Upton House, a boarding establishment."

"Uncle Samuel lived very happily here until his death," Ernestine said. "He was a keen bird-watcher, and as you know, this island is an absolute haven for the blue-toed crane." Again, she paused expectantly.

"Uh—right," Molly said quickly.

"Anyway," Ernestine went on, "to make a long story short, when Uncle Samuel died he left some very peculiar instructions in his will."

"What kind of instructions?" Gwen asked through a mouthful of tart.

"Don't spray crumbs all over the room, girl. Hasn't your mother taught you any manners?" Ethel asked her in a severe voice. Gwen gulped and sat back.

"You see, during the twenty-odd years he lived here, Uncle had filled his rooms with a number of objects: statues, paintings, bookends, even a set of andirons—those metal brackets that hold logs in the fireplace," Ernestine interrupted herself with a wink at Gwen. Then she went on, "Everything followed the theme of birds. Remember, he was a bird enthusiast."

"Right," Molly said, wondering where Ernestine's story was going.

"By the terms of his will, my sisters and I inherited the entire collection of bird art," Ernestine said. "But that wasn't all. Uncle Samuel specified that we must not sell any part of his collection. Instead we must furnish our own rooms with it and keep it with us always. Even when we went on holiday." She took a sip of tea. "Until, that is, we carried out his final wishes."

Edith sniffled and dabbed a hankie to her eyes. "Poor Uncle! All the time we thought he was a wealthy man, and here it turned out he had not a penny to leave us. Just his birds."

"Edith!" Ethel glared. Edith tossed her head.

"So you've been lugging around a bunch of pictures and statues of birds everywhere you go for the last twenty years? That's crazy!" Molly was too astounded to be polite. "Why didn't you just carry out Uncle Samuel's final wishes?"

"Well, you see, that was the trouble," Edith explained. "As far as we knew, Uncle had never told us what his final wishes were."

"But last month, we found out," Ernestine chimed in. "We got a letter from Uncle Samuel."

Molly felt a thrill of excitement. "You mean . . ." She leaned forward. "You mean, a letter from beyond the grave?"

CHAPTER TWO

Gwen nearly choked on a bite of tart.

"Well, not exactly," Ernestine said.

"Ha!" Ethel said. "To be precise, a letter from the dead-letter bin at the post office. Uncle Samuel put the wrong address on it. It had been there for twenty years."

"Twenty years, can you believe it?" Edith chimed in.

"Oh." Molly sat back, disappointed.

"Anyway, the letter contained Uncle Samuel's instructions for a farewell ceremony, here on Blackberry Island," Ernestine said. "So we emptied our savings to come here—"

"*Ernestine!*" Ethel looked furious.

Ernestine clapped her mouth shut. Her face turned beet red.

"We're poor, too," Gwen said cheerfully. "We never have enough customers here. That's why our mother has to work part-time as a lawyer."

The parlor door opened at that moment and the girls' mother walked in. She was a compact, energetic woman with auburn hair and intensely blue eyes. Striding across the room, she shook hands with each of the Biddle sisters in turn.

"I'm Laura O'Brien," she said. "I'm sorry I wasn't here to welcome you, but I hope my husband has seen to your needs."

"Dad threw his back out again," Molly told her mother quickly. "He's lying down in the study."

"Our fault, I'm afraid," Ernestine added.

"Uh-oh," Mrs. O'Brien said. "I'd better see how he is." She smiled around at the Biddle sisters. "I hope you won't mind if Molly and Gwen entertain you for a few moments longer."

"Oh, they're lovely children," Edith said.

Lovely children! Molly squirmed in embarrassment.

Ernestine nodded. "Yes, we've been telling them all about our uncle, Samuel Biddle."

"Samuel Biddle?" Mrs. O'Brien's brows drew together in thought. "That name rings a bell."

"He used to board here," Gwen explained.

Mrs. O'Brien snapped her fingers. "That's right! There's a box full of his old papers and photos in the attic. I found it the other day."

"A box?" Ethel repeated, frowning. "But we inherited everything in his suite. Why weren't the papers sent to us?"

"On the lid it says 'to be burned,'" Mrs. O'Brien said. "I guess he never got around to it before he died, and then no one took care of it later. I meant to have a look through the papers, but I haven't had the chance. However, since you're here—"

"Yes, we'll take them off your hands," Ethel said firmly. She set down her empty teacup. "The box is in the attic, you say?"

"I'll bring it down to your suite," Molly volunteered. The trapdoor to the attic was in her bedroom. The attic was really a little, round, peak-roofed tower that stuck up from the inn like a witch's hat. Molly had wanted the tower itself as her bedroom, but it was too cold and drafty.

"I'll help," Gwen said quickly, and jumped up to follow Molly out of the room. The two girls hurried up to the third floor.

"Boy, they're weird," Gwen said as she helped Molly pull down the ladder to the attic.

Molly shrugged. "I kind of like Ernestine."

"I like Edith better," Gwen said. "But Ethel still gives me the creeps."

Molly climbed into the attic. She immediately spotted the box her mother had mentioned. It was an old wooden fruit crate with SAMUEL BIDDLE written on the side in big black letters.

She hefted it and passed it through the trapdoor to Gwen, who was waiting on the ladder. "Be careful, it's heavy," she warned.

Carrying it between them, the two girls brought the box down to the second floor. The Biddles' suite occupied the northeast corner of the big old house, above the library. Molly knocked on the door and, when she heard Ernestine's voice, pushed it open.

Molly nearly dropped her end of the box when she saw the suite. Earlier that afternoon when she'd aired out the suite and put sheets on the beds, the rooms had looked like any other rooms in the inn, with old but comfortable furniture and a few carefully chosen pictures on the walls.

Now the sitting room was totally transformed. Pictures of birds of every kind covered the walls. A pair of brilliantly painted andirons with heads in the shape of fire-tailed phoenixes were in the fireplace. Matching tongs, poker, and shovel stood on the hearth. On the mantel was a large statue of a wild turkey in full plumage. A tapestry thrown over the small sofa displayed a lone swan in flight over a pond.

Molly stood in the doorway and stared with round eyes. "Wow," she said.

Gwen poked Molly in the back. "Go in, will you," she whispered. "My arms are getting tired."

Molly stepped through the door, and then she and Gwen set the box in front of the sofa. "You carry all this stuff with you every time you go on vacation?" she asked Ernestine.

"Every bit of it," the woman said, nodding.

Behind Ernestine's back, Gwen circled a finger around her ear.

Just then, Ethel strode in from the bedroom, followed by Edith. Edith hurried over to the crate. "What on earth could be in here?" she cried, tearing at the lid with eager fingers.

The lid came off, revealing an untidy stack of yellowed newspaper clippings and a pile of photographs. Molly leaned forward eagerly, but Edith sat back on the sofa with a disappointed sigh.

Ethel snorted. "Edith was convinced Uncle Samuel stashed away his fortune in cash in a fruit crate and left it for us to find," she said.

"I said it was *possible*," Edith retorted.

"When will you believe that there was no fortune?" Ernestine asked. She didn't seem to expect an answer, and she didn't get one.

"Well, let's see what these clippings are." Donning a pair of half-glasses, Ethel sat beside Edith and pulled out a handful of the papers.

As she skimmed the first one, she frowned. "This is an article about Sammy Slick," she said. Turning to the next, her frown deepened. "So is this one. In fact"—she riffled through the rest of the clippings— "they're all about Sammy Slick!"

"How odd," Ernestine said. She perched on the

edge of a chair. "Why would Uncle Samuel collect articles about Sammy Slick?"

"Who *is* Sammy Slick?" Molly asked.

All three sisters gaped at her. "You mean you don't know?" Edith gasped.

"No," Molly replied, bewildered.

"Why, he was just about the most famous gangster who ever lived," Edith declared.

"It started during the Depression, before your time," Ernestine put in kindly. "We were only girls ourselves. Sammy Slick's gang was famous for stealing from the rich and giving to the poor."

"They called him the Robin Hood of Chicago," Edith added.

"He wasn't a *real* gangster, like Al Capone," Ernestine said. "His gang didn't go around killing people or anything like that. Cat burglary was more in their line." She shook her head. "The police never caught any of them. To this day no one knows who Sammy Slick really was."

"Wow," Molly said. Sammy Slick sounded cool!

"Sammy Slick was a hero to some people," Ethel said. "But as Uncle Samuel always said, a thief is a thief."

"That's right," Ernestine agreed, nodding. "When I was twelve I told Uncle I wanted to join Sammy's gang. Sammy had women working for him, you know, even back then. They said his best cat burglar was a woman. That's what I wanted to do. Well, you should have heard the dressing-down Uncle gave me! 'A niece of mine must aspire to be something better than a lawbreaker!' he said. I don't think I ever saw him so angry."

"Uncle was an upright man," Edith said.

"Sammy Slick sounds nicer," Gwen said.

Molly frowned, absently fingering a bookend carved in the shape of an eagle. "It is weird," she said to Ernestine. "Why would your uncle collect articles about a man he detested?"

Ernestine shrugged. "Who knows? He was eccentric, though." Reaching into the wooden crate, she pulled out some of the old photos. "Let's see what else is in here."

Molly leaned over Ernestine's shoulder and studied the topmost photo. It showed a man of about forty-five, with a long, arched nose, dark hair, and a pencil-thin mustache. He was staring into the camera with a startled expression, as if he hadn't expected his picture to be taken. Behind him stood a fair-haired woman with her face turned away from the camera. She had her arm draped over the shoulder of a younger man whose face Molly couldn't make out clearly.

"That's Uncle Samuel," Ernestine said, pointing to the man with the mustache. "I don't know who those others are. Maybe it'll say on the back." She turned the photo over.

"'Sammy and the New Generation, New Year's

Day, 1945,'" Ernestine read aloud.

"'Sammy'?" Ethel looked shocked. "No one ever called Uncle Samuel that. Let me see!"

Sammy? Molly started to get a funny feeling in her stomach. "What about the other pictures?" she asked.

Ernestine held up a second photo. This one showed Samuel Biddle climbing out of a long black car, dressed in a dark overcoat and a private-eye hat, like the kind Sam Spade wore in old movies Molly had seen.

"Oh, my." Ernestine sounded shaken. "What's that in Uncle Samuel's hand?"

Edith leaned over. "Where? I—oh, my. Oh, my!" She stared at Ernestine. "It's a revolver!"

"A revolver?" Ethel echoed, looking stunned.

"Well, maybe he wanted to shoot someone," Gwen suggested.

"Uncle Samuel? Shoot someone?" Edith said.

Molly bit her lip. Her idea had to be right.

Her heart beating faster, she addressed the three old ladies. "I think there's something your Uncle Samuel never told you," she said.

Ethel spoke without a trace of her customary dryness. "What do you mean?"

Molly cleared her throat. "I think your uncle Samuel Biddle and the gangster Sammy Slick were the same person!"

CHAPTER THREE

There was a moment of shocked silence. Then:
"Pshaw!" Ethel asserted.

"Impossible!" Edith declared.

"I think she's right!" Ernestine said, her eyes wide.

"He sure looks like a gangster," Gwen pointed out, holding up the photograph of Uncle Samuel with the gun. "He has a gangster mustache."

"It's the only thing that makes sense. Why else would he keep all these clippings?" Molly tried to speak calmly, though she was bubbling over with excitement. Imagine, a real gangster had lived right here in Welcome Inn. Wait until Josh heard about this!

"A dual identity," Ernestine breathed.

Molly nodded. "Just like Superman!"

"Hardly the happiest comparison," Ethel murmured. Her expression was pinched, as though she had just bitten into a sour apple.

"It's a *good* comparison," Ernestine insisted. "As gangsters go, Sammy Slick was tops. He stole from the rich and gave to the poor." Suddenly her eyes stretched even wider. "And there's more proof. Uncle Samuel was a philanthropist, too!"

Gwen looked confused. "That's what you said before. What is a philanthropist?"

Molly was secretly glad someone else had asked.

"It's someone who does good deeds for other people," Ernestine explained. "Uncle Samuel gave lots of money to charity. And, of course, he supported us after our parents died."

"We always assumed he just gave away his money until there wasn't any left when he died," Edith put in.

"But we never asked where the money *came* from," Ernestine said. She struck a fist into her palm. "How could we have been so naive? We never met any of his business associates. We never went to his office. Good gracious, we never even knew exactly what it was he did!"

"He said he was in business," Ethel murmured. Slowly the shocked look was leaving her face. "We never bothered to find out what sort of business."

Molly spread her hands. "Well, now you know."

"Oh, dear. This is most upsetting." Edith put a hand to her plump cheek. "What will people say?"

"Who cares?" Ernestine let out a laugh. "Oh, Edith, don't take it so badly. I think it's downright thrilling!"

"Ernestine, really!" Ethel shot her sternest glance to her sister.

Ernestine's eyes dropped to her lap. "Well, I do," she muttered stubbornly under her breath.

Ethel sighed. "In answer to your question, Edith, people are not going to say anything, because *we* are not going to say anything. Uncle Samuel's . . . profession . . . is going to remain our secret." Glancing at Molly and Gwen, she added, "Children, would you please leave us now? My sisters and I have matters to discuss."

"Drat, there's the inn phone ringing in the study." Mrs. O'Brien pushed a strand of red-brown hair off her forehead and stirred a big pot on the stove frantically. "Molly, don't just stand there, answer it! If it's someone wanting to have dinner here tonight, tell them we're booked up. I can't cope with a full dining room right now. Oh, why did your father have to throw his back out today?"

Molly hurried into the study. Just as she got there, the phone stopped ringing. She grinned. That took care of that.

Since her husband was in bed, Mrs. O'Brien was

making dinner for the Biddle sisters, the inn's only guests. Fancy cooking was just about the only thing Mrs. O'Brien wasn't a whiz at, and as a result she lost all her usual cool efficiency when she had to do it. The best thing on nights like these, Molly had learned, was to find excuses to stay far away from the kitchen.

Andrew, Molly's older brother, had been the unlucky one chosen to help out tonight. As Molly scurried through the kitchen, she cast a glance at him sitting at the table, peeling potatoes. He caught her look and made a face at her.

Molly refrained from making a face back. Andrew was a horrible brother, but at times like this you could almost feel sorry for him.

"Tell the Biddle sisters dinner will be at seven," Mrs. O'Brien called after Molly, opening the oven. "Oh, no, these birds are *raw*!"

"I'll say seven-thirty," Molly called, and escaped into the dining room.

As she headed for the front stairs, Molly heard Edith Biddle's voice coming from the parlor.

"Dearest, you could have knocked me over with a feather," she was saying. "Sammy Slick, can you imagine? . . . Well, of course! It changes *everything*."

Edith must be on the phone, Molly realized. The O'Briens had just had a separate line installed in the parlor for the guests' use. Molly stuck her head around the slightly open door.

When Edith caught sight of Molly, she gave a violent start. "Hold the line," she said hurriedly. Then, covering the mouthpiece with her hand, she said to Molly, "I'm just, ah, talking to our landlord. About—about taking care of the kitty cat." Her cheeks turned very pink. "Did you want something, dear?" she added.

"Sorry to interrupt." Molly gave her the message about dinner and then withdrew, puzzled. It certainly hadn't sounded as if Edith were talking to the landlord. But why lie about it?

Still puzzling, she went upstairs and raised her hand to knock on the door of the Biddle sisters' suite.

"I'll speak to Edith about the arrangements," Ethel's voice boomed suddenly from the other side of the door. Molly's hand, descending to knock, froze. "In spite of everything, we must go through with it."

Go through with what? Molly wondered.

The door swung open before she could lower her hand. She stood there with it still in the air, feeling silly.

Ethel's hawkish gaze settled on her. "Listening at the door?" she said abruptly.

"Um—" Molly gulped, nervous for no good cause. After all, she had a reason to be there. "I just came to tell you that dinner will be at seven-thirty."

"Thank you." Just as suddenly as she had

opened it, Ethel closed the door in Molly's face.

Gwen was right, Molly decided as she headed for her room on the third floor. The Biddle sisters *were* weird. And another thing: She was starting to get the feeling that Uncle Samuel's true profession wasn't the only secret the sisters were keeping.

Clank!

Molly sat bolt upright in bed. What was that?

"Ernestine!" someone said in a low, furious voice. "You'll wake the whole household if you aren't careful!"

It was dark out. Molly peered at her bedside clock through sleep-clouded eyes. "Five-thirty in the morning," she mumbled. "What's going on?"

"I forgot the instructions," another voice said.

"Well, hurry and get them!"

Now that Molly was starting to wake up a bit, she realized that the voices were coming from outside. Climbing out of bed, she padded across to the open window and peered down. The chill, damp morning air made goosebumps pop out on her skin.

A glow on the rim of the sea, far out to the east, signaled that the sun was about to rise. In the gray half light below, three indistinct figures were moving about. Then the yellow porch light shone briefly on soft silver hair. Molly's eyes widened. It was Edith Biddle!

Edith disappeared into the house. The other two

32

stood waiting for her. One of them—Ernestine, Molly guessed as she saw a red umbrella—shifted a long, strangely shaped object from one shoulder to the other. Molly's lips parted in surprise as she recognized the object. It was a garden spade.

Wasting no more time, Molly flew to her dresser and hauled out a pair of jeans and a flannel shirt. She threw on her clothes and a pair of sneakers. Then, knotting her long, straight dark hair into a ponytail as she went, she raced down to Gwen's room and burst in without knocking.

"Wha—?" Gwen twitched irritably when Molly shook her shoulder. "Go 'way."

"Get up!" Molly ordered. "It's important, Gwen. The Biddle sisters are up to something!"

"Huh?" Gwen sat up in bed.

"They're sneaking away somewhere with a shovel. I want to spy on them."

"But it's the middle of the night," Gwen protested. "You dreamed it, Molly. They're not going anywhere. They're sleeping." She started to lie back down. "So am I."

Molly seized Gwen's wrist. "I didn't dream it. And if we don't hurry they'll be gone and we'll never find them, so get up!" She hauled her sister upright, then crossed to Gwen's closet and threw open the doors.

"Okay, okay." Grumbling, Gwen climbed out of bed. She came up beside Molly and peered into her closet, which was stuffed to bursting with clothes. "Hmm, what should I wear?"

Molly groaned. Gwen was a clothes horse. If she were allowed to think about it, the process of getting dressed could take hours. "Here," she said quickly, pulling out a pair of denim overalls and a hooded sweatshirt.

Gwen frowned. "They don't match."

"Who cares? Spies aren't supposed to be seen, anyway. Now, hurry!"

Seconds later the two girls crept out of Gwen's room and down the back stairs to the kitchen. Molly bit her lip, hoping no one would hear the creaking of the old steps.

She eased open the kitchen door and led Gwen outside. Moving noiselessly in their sneakers, they hurried along the side of the house and peeked around the corner of the porch.

The Biddle sisters were already walking down the steep driveway, shadows in the strange light. The two girls slipped off after them.

"I've never been up this early," Gwen commented in a whisper. "It's so quiet and strange. Where do you think they're going?"

Molly shrugged. "It is the first day of spring, remember. Maybe they're going to do a sunrise ceremony."

Gwen stopped walking. "I thought you said they weren't witches."

"I could have been wrong," Molly conceded.

"I want to go back," Gwen announced.

Molly wished she had kept her mouth shut. "Don't be a baby. Witches aren't necessarily evil, you know."

Gwen said nothing.

"Oh, *please*." The Biddle sisters had crossed the road and were about to disappear into a thicket of pine trees. Molly practically danced up and down, trying to control her impatience. "Look, they probably aren't witches, okay? I'm almost sure they aren't."

Gwen blew out her breath. "Okay."

Grabbing her sister's hand, Molly ran down the driveway, crossed the road, and plunged into the thicket of trees. Coming out the other side, she stopped so suddenly that Gwen smacked into her from behind. The two girls ducked back into the shadow of the trees. Not twenty yards away, the sisters stood conferring.

"It will be waiting for us when we get there," Edith was saying. "I took care of that."

"*If* we get there," Ethel said acidly. "Ernestine, I thought you knew the shortcut."

"Oh, dear, so did I." Ernestine looked worried. "But it's been so long, and all the trees have grown. I think it's over there to the left, just beyond that hill."

"Let's hurry," Ethel said, glancing at the rising sun. "Otherwise we'll miss the sunrise, and the ceremony will be ruined."

Ceremony? Molly felt a chill.

"You better be right about them not being witches, Molly," Gwen whispered. "Come on, they're walking again."

When Molly and Gwen followed the sisters over a rise, Molly felt her throat constrict with nervousness. In front of them was a weathered picket fence with a gate. On the other side of the fence were rows and rows of marble tombstones. It was the back entrance to the Masterman Cemetery.

"A graveyard? Oh, boy," Gwen murmured. "What do we do now?"

Molly swallowed. "We keep going," she answered. "There's nothing to be scared of."

Gwen merely snorted.

The girls slipped through the gate, following the old ladies past a small, reed-fringed pond in which two swans glided. As the light grew stronger, Molly saw the Biddle sisters halt at a gloomy marble angel on a column. Tall letters on it spelled out the name SAMUEL BIDDLE. Molly led Gwen to a nearby tombstone, behind which they both crouched.

Suddenly Gwen tugged on Molly's arm and pointed, round-eyed. Molly followed her sister's finger. Her own eyes widened as she caught sight of a man-sized, canvas-covered shape standing next to the marble angel.

"What is it?" Gwen asked in a trembling

whisper. "Is it . . . is it a body?"

Molly was afraid to even guess. But now Edith had pulled a piece of paper out of her purse. "Shh!" Molly said. "Something's happening."

Unfolding the piece of paper, Edith began to read. "Face the angel, two feet away," she directed. "Then take six paces to the left."

Ernestine did as Edith said. "Big paces," Ethel advised. "Remember, he was a tall man."

"Who was tall?" Gwen whispered. "The guy under that canvas sheet, maybe?"

"Pivot left and step one and a half paces to the right," Edith read. "Goodness, how precise!"

"Go on," Ernestine said. "It's getting late."

"Line up the tomb of Henry Kravis with the obelisk of Dorcas Worthy," Edith read. "Take one pace in that direction. Dig."

Molly and Gwen stared at each other in horror. Dig? In a graveyard, at sunrise?

"Are they going to bury someone, or are they going to dig someone up?" Molly whispered.

"They're *worse* than witches," Gwen said.

Both girls' eyes were riveted on Ernestine's untidy figure. She handed her red umbrella to Ethel. And then, as the sun heaved clear of the horizon, she swung the spade down till the blade bit into the earth.

CHAPTER FOUR

Ernestine grunted slightly with effort as she tossed the spadeful of sod aside. *Chunk!* The shovel thudded into the ground again. Pulling a gardening fork out of one of her poncho pockets, Ethel knelt and started digging with her sister.

Edith took a seat on a nearby headstone. "Ah, the country! The air is lovely," she chirped. "And it's so quiet. And those handsome swans! What a wonderful way to begin a spring day!"

Molly, behind the tombstone, raised her eyebrows.

Ernestine's cheeks began to turn pink as she dug. "The soil is nice and loose," she said, sounding a little breathless.

"Mmm. Plenty of worms to keep it soft," Ethel

answered. She stabbed her fork into the ground with a twisting motion. "Useful creatures, worms."

Molly clapped a hand over Gwen's mouth to keep her from letting out a squeal.

Ching! Suddenly the spade struck something metallic. Ernestine straightened up with an anxious expression. "Oh, dear, there's something here already," she said, casting a glance around at the headstones. "How awkward."

"Dig it up and let's see," Ethel said.

Ernestine resumed her efforts. A moment later she said, "I can see metal!"

"Here, let me," Ethel said. Bending over the hole, she attacked it with the gardening fork. After a few moments, Molly saw her reach down and pull out a small, flat box.

She frowned. "Looks like a strongbox."

Edith gave an excited cry. "Let me see!"

"A strongbox?" Ernestine repeated.

"I wonder what's in it," Gwen whispered, her fright all but forgotten in her curiosity.

"Me, too," Molly agreed, fascinated.

"Open it," Edith urged.

"Girls!" Ethel said sternly. "We came here for a purpose. Whatever's in the box, it can wait until we've done what we came to do."

"Uh-oh. Here comes the witches' ceremony," Gwen murmured.

"Ernestine, bring the ash," Ethel commanded.

39

The ash? Molly stared as Ernestine, groaning and puffing, carried the shrouded object to the hole she'd dug. If that was just the ashes of something, whatever it was must have been huge!

Then Ernestine whipped the canvas off the object. Molly nearly choked.

It was a tree!

"Lovely," Ethel said approvingly. "A fine young ash. Uncle Samuel couldn't ask for better."

Molly's jaw dropped as she realized what this was all about. This was the farewell ceremony the sisters had mentioned. It was their memorial for Uncle Samuel. And she and Gwen had thought it was a witches' ritual!

Ethel nodded. "Lower it in, Ernestine."

Obediently, Ernestine set the young ash tree in the hole. She shoveled back the earth she'd removed, then set the chunks of sod carefully on top and tamped them down.

"A moment of silence," Ethel said. The three sisters bowed their heads in the bright sun.

Ernestine looked up and rubbed her hands briskly. "Well," she said. "That's that. We planted the ash tree at sunrise, just as Uncle Samuel asked in his final letter."

"Now for that strongbox," Edith added.

"It isn't ours," Ethel objected.

But Ernestine replied with sudden firmness, "It is ours, Ethel. Uncle Samuel meant for us to find it.

It makes sense. Why else would he have left such specific instructions about where to plant his ash tree?"

"I'd hardly say it makes sense," Ethel snapped. "It's very odd, if you ask me. Why would Uncle Samuel bury a strongbox in a cemetery?"

"I'm sure he had his reasons," Ernestine pointed out. "Don't forget, he was a gangster."

"Must you remind me?" Ethel sighed.

"Girls!" Edith cried impatiently. "Don't you see? It must be Uncle Samuel's missing money!"

Molly caught her breath. Edith could be right! Samuel Biddle, respectable businessman, would never bury a fortune in a cemetery—but the gangster Sammy Slick might very well!

Ethel said nothing, but her nostrils flared. After a moment she nodded her head. "All right."

Ernestine set the box on a tombstone and tried the lid. "It isn't locked."

"Hurry," Edith urged. "Open it!"

Ernestine looked at Ethel, then flung back the lid. The three sisters crowded close around the box. Molly and Gwen craned their necks, wishing they could see better.

Edith groaned. "It isn't money," she said. "It's another letter from Uncle Samuel."

"It's addressed to us," Ethel noted.

"There's a key, too," Ernestine said. She held aloft a large brass skeleton key.

Ethel pulled out the letter and unfolded it. As she skimmed the page, her brows drew together over her beaky nose. "Why, it's gibberish," she said angrily, looking up. "These aren't even words. They're random collections of letters."

"Maybe it's a code," Molly whispered excitedly. She'd recently read a book about codes.

"Oh, poor Uncle," Edith said. "He must have been more ill than we realized. His wits must have been addled when he wrote this!"

"Or it's a practical joke," Ethel muttered.

Ernestine coughed. "Uncle Samuel didn't have much of a sense of humor," she pointed out.

Ethel raised a bony hand. "I've had enough of this. I want my breakfast. Let's go back to the inn, girls."

Molly and Gwen waited until the sisters had vanished over the crest of the hill before they came out from their hiding place. Molly's brown eyes were shining.

"You know what this means, don't you?" she asked Gwen.

"What what means?" Gwen asked. Then she looked more closely at her older sister. Her eyes narrowed. "Oh, no. Not again."

"Oh, yes," Molly said. "We just found ourselves an adventure!"

At ten o'clock that morning, Molly marched up

to the Biddle sisters' suite and rapped boldly on their door. She'd thought a lot about her idea, and she had made up her mind.

"They aren't going to like it," Gwen warned from right behind her.

"Just let me handle it," Molly said.

"That's how it always starts," Gwen said, sighing. "And before it's over we're always in big trouble."

The door swung open and Ernestine peered out. "Why, hello, girls," she said, her wrinkled face breaking into a smile. "Won't you come in?"

"Thanks." Molly stepped into the sitting room and smiled a bit nervously at Edith and Ethel, who were seated in the two chairs by the fireplace.

Ethel looked annoyed. "What is it, children? We're in the middle of an important discussion."

"We know," Molly said. "That's why we're here."

Ethel raised one eyebrow. "I'm afraid I don't understand what you mean."

Molly took a deep breath. "We followed you to the cemetery this morning," she blurted out.

"I declare!" Edith said, looking shocked. "Children's manners aren't what they used to be."

"They certainly aren't," Ethel agreed grimly.

"I told you they'd be mad," Gwen murmured.

Even Ernestine looked startled. "Why did you follow us?" she asked.

"We thought you were w—" Gwen began to say.

Molly interrupted. "We thought you were, uh, wandering around and might get lost," she improvised hastily. "And we were curious," she added, seeing Ethel's skeptical stare.

"I see," Ethel said, frowning. "Well, so you followed us. You saw us plant Uncle's tree."

"And we saw you dig up the box," Gwen added.

"What of it?"

"Well, it's just . . ." Molly paused, unsure how to go on. Walking over to the fireplace, she picked up the red-and-purple phoenix poker from its stand and hefted it absently. It was very heavy. Its glittering green eyes gazed at her.

"Don't fidget, child," Ethel scolded.

"I just polished that, and now you're getting fingerprints all over it," Edith added.

"Sorry." Molly put the poker back and stuffed her hands into her pockets.

"Spit it out, dear," Ernestine advised.

"Okay. We have a proposition to make. See, you may not realize it, but a skeleton key hidden in a box buried in a cemetery means only one thing," Molly said in a rush. "It means adventure."

"It means nothing of the kind," Ethel said.

"Ethel, hear the child out," Ernestine said. Her old eyes were bright with curiosity.

Molly clasped her hands together. "I know we're only kids, but Gwen and I have had a lot of experience with adventures. Really, we have. Once we found a box of pirate treasure, and once we solved a hundred-year-old murder mystery. We might be able to help you with your adventure, too."

Falling silent, she gazed anxiously at the three old ladies. Edith's face was blank with surprise. Ethel's frown drew the corners of her mouth down into an upside-down U. But Ernestine was smiling eagerly.

"Oh, that's wonderful!" she said.

Ethel stirred and rose to her feet. "I think this nonsense has gone on long enough," she said. "It's understandable when children let their imaginations run away with them, but Ernestine, you are seventy-one years old. You have no excuse. The buried case was Uncle Samuel's little joke, and that's that."

"No," Molly insisted. "Your uncle *couldn't* have gone to all that trouble just for a practical joke. And what about the letter he left you?"

"It's gibberish," Edith explained.

"Molly says it isn't," Gwen said. "She thinks it's a code."

Ethel made an impatient gesture. "Ridiculous. Why would Uncle Samuel leave us a coded letter?"

"I'm not sure," Molly said. "But he could have had lots of reasons. Don't forget, he was also the gangster Sammy Slick."

"Between you and Ernestine, I'm not likely to

forget," Ethel snapped. But her expression was growing doubtful.

"Oh, Ethel, give in." Ernestine spoke up. "Can't you see? The children are right! Even if it leads to nothing, we must try to understand what Uncle Samuel meant to tell us. It's our duty."

"I agree," Edith said unexpectedly.

"Hmmph." Ethel snorted.

"And goodness knows we have no understanding about codes or that sort of thing," Ernestine went on. "If we're to pursue it, we need the help of a couple of experienced adventurers."

Molly smiled gratefully at Ernestine.

Ethel threw her hands up. "Oh, all right," she grumbled. "I still say it's ridiculous, but far be it from me to stop you from having your fun, Ernestine."

"All right!" Gwen cheered. In her excitement, she had clearly forgotten to worry about getting into trouble.

Molly's grin spread from ear to ear. "So I guess we have a deal," she said, holding out her hand to Ernestine.

"Deal!" Ernestine shook hands heartily.

"Deal," echoed Edith, smiling.

"Deal," Ethel agreed gloomily. "Hmmph!"

CHAPTER FIVE

"The first thing we all have to do is swear not to tell anyone else about the strongbox," Molly said briskly.

Ernestine was delighted. "Shall we swear in blood? I've got a needle in my sewing kit."

Ethel closed her eyes in resignation.

Molly was tempted until she glanced at Gwen, who was faintly green. "Uh—I think we can just give our word," she said quickly.

"Goodness, why ever do we need to be so secretive?" Edith asked.

Molly was a little taken aback. "Well, because, because . . ." she began.

Ernestine came to her rescue. "Heavens, Edith, don't you know anything about adventures? That's how it's done," she said severely. "Besides, I'm sure all the ex-members of the gang are after Uncle's money, too. We want to make sure they don't get wind of what we've discovered."

"Right!" Molly said gratefully.

"Oh, rubbish," Ethel said. "Not that I believe any of this foolishness anyway, but surely you're not worried about Uncle Samuel's colleagues finding out about the strongbox? Uncle Samuel died twenty years ago at the age of seventy-four. I'm sure his associates are long dead now, too."

Molly was crestfallen. She hadn't thought of that.

"Maybe not!" Ernestine said triumphantly. "In the New Year's picture we saw, there were some young people. The 'New Generation,' it said. Those people probably aren't much older than we are, Ethel. They could still be around."

"Yeah!" Molly agreed, brightening.

"But it hardly seems likely that they'd be lingering here so many years later," Edith pointed out. "Whatever Uncle was trying to hide, it can't have been that important."

Crushed again, Molly nodded. "You're right."

"Well, what should we do next?" Ernestine asked. "I suppose you'll want to see the note Uncle Samuel left in the box?"

Ethel reached into the pocket of her shapeless black cardigan and handed a yellowed piece of paper to Molly, who eagerly began to read it.

JY NBSP BREBI, BNFRE, SKN BPKBQRFKB:
F HKLV RESR YLT VFII CFKN FK YLTPQBIUBQ
REB QMFPFR LC SNUBKRTPB YLT VFII KBBN
RL QLIUB JY MTZZIB.

Her heart sank. There was close to a page of this mess. However was she going to decipher it?

"Uh—great," she said, trying to smile. "It looks like a code to me."

Ethel folded her arms. "You have no idea how to read it, do you?" she asked.

"Ethel!" Ernestine said reproachfully. "Molly knows what she's doing. Why, she's probably already figured out what the note really says, haven't you, dear?" She smiled at Molly.

Molly squirmed. "Well, I haven't got quite that far," she hedged. "But I have some ideas."

"Oh, good! You've got your thinking cap on," Edith said. Turning to her sisters, she clasped her hands. "Aren't they clever girls to be able to read codes? It makes me wish I were a child again myself. Well, come along, Ethel, Ernestine. Let's take a walk so the children can work in peace."

In a flurry of shawls, ponchos, and one red umbrella, the sisters swept out of the suite, leaving Molly and Gwen staring after them with their mouths open.

Gwen blinked. "Are they leaving us to do all the work on our own?" she asked.

"It looks that way," Molly said. Slumping down on the sofa, she stared moodily at the statue of the wild turkey. "Maybe it's just as well," she added. "That way they won't be around to watch me make a fool of myself."

By noon, Molly and Gwen had made little headway on Sammy Slick's message. They were concentrating on the first sentence. If they could figure out how to read that, Molly hoped, they'd have a basis for deciphering the rest of the page.

They replaced all the *B*'s in the sentence with *E*'s. They did this because there were more *B*'s than any other letter in the message, and Molly had read in her book of codes that *E* was the most commonly used letter in the English language.

But after that they were stumped. This is what they had:

JY NeSP eREeI, eNFRE, SKN ePKeQRFKe:
F HKLV RESR YLT VFII CFKN FK
YLTPQeIUeQ REe QMFPFR LC SNUeKRTPe
YLT VFII KeeN RL QLIUe JY MTZZIe.

"'Ereei, enfre, skn epkeqrfke.' It's still gibberish," Gwen said. "But the three *E*'s kind of give it a rhythm. Like 'ally, ally in-free.'"

"Oh, be quiet," Molly snapped. She was feeling extremely grumpy.

"I'm hungry," Gwen said.

Molly stood up, brushing pink crumbs of eraser off her lap. "Me, too. Let's go have lunch. We can try the code again later."

As they went down the back stairs, they heard a deep, hearty voice in the kitchen.

Molly's scowl eased. "Grandpa Lloyd!" she said, running down the rest of the steps.

"Grandpa Lloyd!" Gwen echoed.

The white-bearded man at the kitchen table turned his blue eyes toward the girls. "Well, hello there, youngsters," he said, smiling.

Grandpa Lloyd was one of Molly's favorite people. He'd lived on Blackberry Island all his life, and knew more of its stories and legends than anyone else. He lived in his own house in the village, but since the O'Briens had bought Welcome Inn, he spent more time there than at home. It was a lucky thing, too, Molly's father often said, because Grandpa Lloyd was the only one in the family who knew anything about keeping an old, run-down house together.

He also knew how to cook. "Ned Halleck gave me a mess of fresh clams this morning," he was saying to Mrs. O'Brien. "What else could I do but make clam chowder? And I *had* to bring the stuff to you. I'd never eat it all before it spoiled."

"Dad," their mother replied. "I know you made the chowder to stop me from going crazy trying to cook for the guests. And the biscuits, too. Just stop fibbing and help me get it ready to serve. And when the Biddle sisters rave about how good the food is, keep your mouth shut and let me take the credit." She grinned.

"The Biddle sisters?" Grandpa Lloyd repeated. "Not old Samuel Biddle's three nieces?"

"The same," Mrs. O'Brien confirmed. "They're in the parlor now. They're here for some sort of memorial ceremony for their uncle."

"Well, I'll be." Grandpa Lloyd stroked his beard. "Ethel, Ernestine, and Edith. Used to see them birdwatching with their uncle in the summers. Edith was pretty, as I recall." He rose casually to his feet. "I guess it'd be unfriendly not to go in and say hello."

Mrs. O'Brien laughed. "Go ahead, you old flirt. But don't get your hopes up. From what Ernestine has told me, Edith had one great love, but he jilted her about fifty years ago. She's sworn off men since then."

As Grandpa Lloyd left the room, Molly thought of the phone conversation she'd overheard the night before. Edith had called the person she was talking to "dearest." Maybe she had finally gotten over her great love. It certainly had sounded as if she had a new boyfriend now.

"Here, girls." Mrs. O'Brien handed each of her daughters a bowl of the steaming, savory chowder. "Be my food testers."

"Mmm! It's really good," Gwen mumbled through a mouthful. "So're the biscuits."

Molly said nothing. She was too busy spooning up soup.

When the girls finished eating, they set up a buffet in the dining room. Then Gwen went to the parlor and announced lunch to the guests.

Grandpa Lloyd ushered the three old ladies into the dining room, still chatting. "Oh, yes, Kitty Upton," he was saying. He pulled out a chair for Ethel. "She sold Upton House and retired right after your uncle passed away. She still lives on the island, though, over on Beachy Lane."

"Fancy that," Edith said. "Perhaps we ought to visit her."

"Hmmph!" Ethel shook out her napkin with a flick. "I never cared for Kitty Upton, and I doubt she cared for us, either. I don't think we need bother with her."

Molly went into the kitchen and got the basket of biscuits her mother had just finished warming. Covering them with a cloth, she carried them out to the buffet.

"Well, I'd better be off," Grandpa Lloyd said. "Nice seeing you ladies again. Ethel, Edith, and Ernestine—the three *E*'s." He gazed around the dining room. "Brings back memories of the way this place used to be."

Molly's hand froze in the act of setting the biscuits down. The three *E*'s . . .

Then she let out an excited yelp. "The three *E*'s! Maybe that's it!"

Four uncomprehending faces turned toward her. "Would you like to say something?" Ethel asked with a disapproving frown.

"No, thank you," Molly said hastily. "I just thought of something, that's all." She was backing toward the doorway as she spoke. "Excuse me."

Then she was in the kitchen. Grabbing Gwen by the arm, she raced upstairs to the Biddle suite as fast as she could go.

Half an hour later, Molly put down her pencil and nodded with satisfaction. "Okay. The first sentence gives us enough letters to decipher the whole page."

"And I was the one who figured it out!" Gwen crowed. "If I hadn't noticed the three *E*'s in the first sentence, we'd never have cracked the code."

Molly rolled her eyes. It was true, Gwen had given her the idea, but she was getting tired of hearing about it.

The breakthrough had come when Molly suddenly realized that the three words that began with *E* in the first line of the message might be the names Ethel, Edith, and Ernestine. Each had the right number of letters. When she and Gwen had substituted the letters in those names for the letters on the page, they'd ended up with this:

JY deSr ethel, edith, Snd ernestine:

i HnLV thSt YLT Vill Cind in YLTrselUes the sMirit LC SdUentTre YLT Vill need tL sLlUe JY MTZZle.

From there, the girls were able to guess at some of the other letters until, bit by bit, they deciphered the entire sentence.

"Let's hurry and do the rest," Molly said. "You take the first paragraph, I'll take the second. I made you a copy with the key written at the bottom." She handed Gwen a piece of paper. "The capital letters are the code, and the small letters are the key. All you have to do is change the key letters for the code letters."

Fifteen minutes later, Molly and Gwen stopped to compare notes. As they put the pieces of the deciphered message together and took in their meaning, Molly's brown eyes grew round.

"Gwen, go get the Biddle sisters," she said. "I think we better have a meeting."

"Yeah," Gwen agreed, and left the room.

A few moments later, the ladies arrived. "What's this about?" Ethel asked.

"We cracked the code," Molly announced.

Ethel's eyebrows shot up.

"Oh, I knew you would!" Ernestine said, clapping her hands.

"What does the message say?" Edith asked.

"I'll read it to you. But I think you better sit down," Molly advised.

Exchanging startled glances, the ladies sat.

Suppressing a shiver of excitement, Molly picked up her notebook and cleared her throat.

"'My dear Ethel, Edith, and Ernestine,'" she read. "'I know that you will find in yourselves the spirit of adventure you will need to solve my puzzle.

"'I have chosen this unorthodox means of communication of necessity. I cannot turn my estate over to the authorities because it would raise too many unfortunate questions (though I wish to assure you that every cent I leave to you was gained by legitimate means). And I do not trust my former colleagues. In fact, it is out of fear that they will seek to cheat you that I have taken such extreme measures.'"

"Oh, my," Edith murmured. She was pale with excitement. "I wonder what Uncle is driving at?"

"Shh!" Ethel ordered. "Let the girl go on."

Molly continued. "'Rest assured, dear nieces, that I have made provision for you, as I always promised. But to safeguard your fortune, I have had to conceal it. Therefore, I have left a series of clues that you and only you will be able to understand. Just follow the trail, girls. Answer my riddles and the money is yours!'"

CHAPTER SIX

Ethel's mouth was open in shock. When Molly stopped reading, she asked, "Are you sure you deciphered the note correctly?" She seemed dazed.

"We're sure," Molly said.

"It was all because of me," Gwen boasted.

Molly glared at her sister. Of all the nerve!

Edith let out a cry of delight. Jumping up, she threw her arms around a startled Gwen. "Oh, you dear, dear child," she caroled. "Thank you! I *knew* Uncle Samuel couldn't leave us to starve."

As Gwen disentangled herself, Molly cautioned, "Don't forget, he meant you to get this note twenty years ago. Someone else might have found the money by now. Especially if the members of his gang were really as crooked as he says."

"As he also said, more than once, a thief is a thief," Ethel murmured hollowly.

"Oh, but surely Uncle would have taken precautions," Ernestine said. A wide smile broke across her face. "Girls, isn't it thrilling? Follow the trail! Answer the riddle! We're really going to have an adventure!"

Molly expected Ethel to quell her twin with a sharp word, but for once the eldest Biddle sister seemed at a loss. She simply sat there shaking her head. "Unbelievable," she muttered. "It's like waking up and finding oneself in a dime novel."

Ernestine grasped Molly's hand. "Is there more?" she asked eagerly. "*Did* Uncle Samuel leave us a riddle?"

Molly nodded and picked up her notebook again. "We couldn't figure it out, but maybe you'll know what it means."

I stalk upon stilts, looking down from the skies.
In a storm-colored coat I fool enemy eyes.
With me always are scissors, with which I eat fish.
Find me at home and I'll grant you your wish.

Molly lowered the notebook. The ladies were staring blankly at her.

"Scissors?" Edith said. "I've heard of fish knives, but who ever heard of eating fish with *scissors*?"

"Perhaps that's how gangsters do it," Ethel suggested sourly. "*I* certainly wouldn't know."

Even Ernestine was downcast. "I don't know anyone who walks on stilts, either. I suppose we could try the circuses."

Molly shook her head. They didn't get it!

"I don't think you're looking at it the right way," she said. "You're not meant to take riddles literally. They're supposed to show something to you, in a poetic kind of way."

"That one shows me nothing," Ethel said firmly.

Edith fluttered her hands. "I never was very good at games like that."

"I'm stumped," Ernestine said.

Molly pressed her lips together to hold back her disappointment. "Well, maybe you should keep on thinking about it," she suggested.

"Yeah. Concentrate!" Gwen urged. "You want your wish to be granted, don't you?"

Ernestine smiled. "We'll certainly try."

"Okay, well . . ." Molly trailed off, shrugging. There was nothing more she or Gwen could do. "I guess we'll leave you alone to think," she said.

From the armchair came Ethel's familiar snort. "At last!"

Molly walked out onto the front porch and kicked moodily at the leg of the glider.

Gwen followed her. "Do you think they'll figure

out the answer to the riddle?" she asked.

Molly scowled. "I don't know. They sure don't seem to be trying very hard." Leaning on the porch rail, she gazed out at the Atlantic Ocean. It was a perfect spring day; a breeze with just a hint of chill blew in off the waves, and puffy white clouds wandered across the deep blue of the sky.

"It's so frustrating!" Molly burst out after a moment. "Here we are with this great clue, and the Biddle sisters are the only ones who can tell us what it means. They're the only ones who knew Sammy Slick well enough to figure out what he might have meant."

"Maybe we could do something else," Gwen said.

Molly glanced at her sister. "Something else like what?"

"I don't know. Like finding out what we can about Sammy Slick on our own."

Molly narrowed her eyes in thought. "Yeah," she said slowly. "That's not a bad idea, Gwen."

"It isn't?" Gwen looked pleased.

"No." Molly snapped her fingers. "In fact, it's a good idea. Did you hear when Grandpa Lloyd told the Biddles that Kitty Upton, the lady who ran Upton House, still lives on the island?"

Gwen nodded.

"Well, who else besides his nieces would know something about Samuel Biddle, also known as

Sammy Slick?" Molly asked. "His landlady, that's who! So let's go find Kitty Upton."

"Okay!" Gwen's blue eyes shone with pride. "Hey, Molly, that's two good ideas I had today. First the three E's, now Kitty Upton."

"Yeah, well, don't let it go to your head," Molly muttered. She was getting tired of Gwen taking all the credit.

Molly ran inside and grabbed the phone book. Flipping to U, she ran her finger down the few entries. There were only two Uptons, a D. Upton on Oak Street and a T. Upton on Beachy Lane. "Grandpa said she lives on Beachy Lane, so that has to be it. I guess Kitty's her nickname," Molly mused. Raising her voice, she called, "Gwen! Let's go!"

Beachy Lane was on a narrow neck of land near the ferry harbor. Most of the people who had houses there were rich weekenders. Kitty Upton was one of the few full-time residents. At her small, modern one-story house the girls got off their bikes and went up the flagstone path to the front door. Molly pressed the bell.

"Just a minute!" a woman's voice called from inside.

"What are we going to say?" Gwen whispered as they waited for the door to open.

"We can't tell her the real reason we're asking all these questions. We're sworn to secrecy about that. So we'll have to make up a reason," Molly replied.

"Just let me do the talking, okay?"

Gwen pouted. "You're jealous because I'm the one who's had all the good ideas today."

Molly rolled her eyes. But before she could answer, the door swung open. A small, thin elderly woman stood gazing at them. Everything about her was tense and taut. Her gray hair was curled into a tight permanent; the skin of her narrow face was stretched over her bones, and her lips were compressed into a thin, suspicious line.

"Yes?" she said.

Gazing at her, Molly suddenly discovered that she had no idea what her cover story should be. She gulped. "Um—Mrs. Upton?"

"That's right. What do you want?"

Molly introduced herself and Gwen, who was still pouting. "We live in Welcome Inn," she added. "The place that used to be Upton House."

Kitty Upton folded her arms. "And?"

"And . . ." Molly shifted her feet, feeling a little desperate. "We're doing a project." Yes, that was good! "About, uh, local philanthropists." Good, she hadn't stumbled over the word. "We're trying to find out more about Samuel Biddle. We heard he was one of your boarders at Upton House."

Kitty Upton's lips compressed even more.

"We already found out some neat stuff," Gwen said suddenly. "Did you know that he was really the famous gangster Sammy Slick?"

Molly clenched her teeth, furious. Gwen and her big mouth!

But a spark of interest showed for the first time in Kitty Upton's pale blue eyes. "You don't say?" she said. "Samuel Biddle?"

Gwen nodded. "Yes," she said. "It's true. We found a bunch of old pictures and clippings in a box in the attic."

"Really? My stars. Samuel Biddle, of all people, a gangster! What do you know?" Stepping back, Kitty Upton held open the door. "Why don't you girls come in?"

"Thanks!" Gwen said, flashing Molly a look of smug triumph.

Though still annoyed, Molly had to admit that maybe Gwen had had the right idea after all. Kitty Upton seemed to be interested. If telling her about Sammy Slick would get her to talk to them, maybe it wasn't such a bad thing.

The girls followed Kitty Upton through a dark hallway that smelled of furniture polish and disinfectant. Glancing into a room as they passed, Molly caught a glimpse of slipcovered, plain-looking beige furniture.

Then they were in the kitchen, and Kitty Upton was inviting them to sit. A middle-aged man stood with his hand on the knob of the back door. He had fair hair and the same pale blue eyes as Kitty Upton.

"My son, Donald Junior," she said.

"Hi, kids," the man said. "Mother, I've got to run. I'm going up to Rocky Point to meet with the construction foreman."

"On a Sunday?" Kitty Upton looked disapproving.

Molly and Gwen sneaked glances at each other. Donald Upton must work for the company that was building the new condos at Rocky Point. It was a good thing their mother wasn't with them, Molly thought. Mrs. O'Brien was one of the most determined opponents of the project.

"Don, the girls have the most interesting news," Kitty Upton said. "They say my old boarder Samuel Biddle was really that gangster Sammy Slick!"

Donald Upton took his hand off the doorknob. He looked shocked. "Well, well!"

Kitty Upton pursed her lips primly. "When I think of how he acted like such a fine gentleman," she said. "A pillar of the community! On the board of every charity! Oh, he had plenty of money to throw around. Spent the stuff like it was water, on all sorts of useless things like art. Pictures of birds. Andirons, for heaven's sake, even though the fireplace in his room didn't work. And all the time he was just a common crook."

"Say," Donald Upton broke in, "how did you kids find out about this, anyway? I always heard that no one ever knew Slick's true identity."

Molly and Gwen told him about the box full of clippings and photos from the attic.

Upton raised his eyebrows. "Photos? I'll bet there are other gang members in those pictures. Have you shown them to the police?"

"No. You can't really see anyone except Sammy Slick," Molly explained. "Most of the other faces are pretty blurry."

"Besides," Gwen added, "we kind of want to keep it a secret. The Biddle sisters are sort of embarrassed that their uncle turned out to be a gangster. They're staying with us, you see."

Upton nodded. "I see. Well, I guess finding out who the other members of the gang were doesn't matter much after all these years, anyway."

Kitty Upton's pale eyes were frankly malicious. "Those high-and-mighty nieces of his must be embarrassed! Why, those girls thought they were royalty. Especially that Edith, mincing around with her nose in the air, flirting with all the young men, stealing other people's beaus."

Molly squirmed in her seat, embarrassed by Kitty Upton's outburst and dismayed to hear the Biddle sisters talked about in such a way. She wished Gwen had never brought them up.

"Mother," Donald Upton said, chuckling a bit uncomfortably. "That's enough!" To the girls, he added, "My mother's tired. She hasn't been well. Maybe you should go now."

"But—" Gwen began.

Molly kicked her sister under the table. "Yeah,

we better go," she agreed. "Uh—thanks."

Outside, Molly stomped down the path and flipped up the kickstand on her bike. Gwen scowled at her. "Why did you kick me? I was going to ask some more questions."

"You were going to *ask* some more questions?" Molly repeated furiously. "Gwen, you didn't *ask* any questions. You just answered them. We swore this morning that we wouldn't tell anyone about Sammy Slick, and already you're spilling the beans to the whole wide world!"

"We *didn't* swear we wouldn't tell anyone about Sammy Slick," Gwen argued, her voice rising. "We just swore we wouldn't tell about the strongbox. There's a difference!"

"*Shhh!*" Molly hissed. She looked around, but there was no one in sight but themselves.

"You're just jealous because I'm better at figuring out stuff," Gwen said.

Gritting her teeth, Molly climbed on her bike. "Just shut up and ride," she muttered. "Let's go home before the whole world finds out about Sammy Slick's fortune."

"There you are," Mrs. O'Brien exclaimed when Molly and Gwen walked into the kitchen at Welcome Inn. "I was starting to worry about you girls. It's nearly five o'clock."

"Sorry," Molly said. She reached for a chair at

the same moment as Gwen. They had a brief, silent struggle, which Molly won. Her face contracted in a fierce scowl, Gwen flung herself into a chair on the other side of the table.

"Uh-oh," Mrs. O'Brien said, looking from Gwen to Molly. "Who started it?"

"Molly told me to shut up," Gwen burst out. Her lower lip started to tremble.

"Is that true?" Mrs. O'Brien asked Molly.

Molly tossed her head in disdain. If Gwen was going to be a tattletale, let her. Molly had more guts than to turn to her parents to resolve a fight.

Mrs. O'Brien waited. When it became clear that Molly wasn't going to say anything, she said, "Molly, you know better than to speak to your sister that way. Don't you think you should apologize?"

"No," Molly said stonily. Apologize to that crybaby? Never!

Mrs. O'Brien sighed. "Well, then, I guess you'd better go to your room and think it over."

As usual, Molly thought bitterly, she was getting the blame. "Fine," she muttered. Pushing back her chair, she stalked out of the kitchen and headed up the front stairs.

As she reached the top of the stairs, a door at the far end of the hall flew open and a gray head popped out. "There you are!" Ernestine exclaimed. "I've been looking all over for you!"

Molly paused. She wasn't in the mood for the three old ladies right now. "What for?" she asked.

Ernestine scurried down the hall, her eyes gleaming with eagerness.

"It's the riddle," she whispered, taking Molly by the arm. "Edith solved it!"

CHAPTER SEVEN

"Are you serious?" Molly exclaimed, forgetting her bad mood in an instant.

"Quite," Ernestine assured her happily. "And what's more, we think we know where to look for the money!"

"Molly!" Mrs. O'Brien called up the stairs. "Go to your room, please."

Oh, no! Molly groaned inwardly. She'd forgotten about that. To be grounded now, of all times!

She hesitated only a second over the painful decision. Then she detached Ernestine's wrinkled hand from her arm.

"Wait right here," she said. "Please." And she ran back down the stairs.

Bursting into the kitchen, she faced her mother.

"I thought about it," she said breathlessly. Turning to Gwen, she announced, "I'm sorry I told you to shut up, Gwen. *Really* sorry. I won't do it again."

"Oh. Oh, well—" Gwen faltered, confused.

"What's gotten into you?" her mother demanded.

"I just changed my mind. Can I be excused now?" Molly asked.

"But—" her mother began. Then she shrugged. "Never mind. I'm not going to look a gift horse in the mouth. All right, go on. Do whatever you're about to do."

"Thanks." Flashing a smile, Molly turned and pounded back up the stairs.

Ernestine still stood where Molly had left her, looking bewildered. "What happened?" she asked.

"It's a long story," Molly said. She headed toward the suite. "I want to hear about how you solved the riddle."

"Oh, dear. I don't think you should go in there right now," Ernestine said, hurrying ahead of Molly to block the door.

"Why not?" Molly asked, confused.

Ernestine looked distressed. "You see, Edith was so pleased with herself for having guessed the answer to Uncle's riddle, she *wouldn't* stop crowing, and—well, to make a long story short, Ethel and she had a fight, and now Edith is crying and Ethel's lying down with a migraine headache."

Molly's jaw dropped. "You have arguments, too?" she said incredulously. "But you guys are grown-ups!"

"Some things never change, I'm afraid," Ernestine said with an apologetic smile.

"I guess not," Molly murmured. After a moment, she looked up at Ernestine. "Well, it's up to you and me, then. Come on, let's go. We only have an hour before it gets dark."

"Where are we going?" Ernestine asked.

Molly grinned. "To the place that's the answer to the riddle."

"A—alone?" Ernestine faltered. "Without any of the others?"

Molly shrugged. "No one else really seems to want to have this adventure but us. So let's go have it by ourselves."

After a moment Ernestine gave a delighted chuckle. "I'll just get my things," she said. "Don't go away."

Ten minutes later Molly and Ernestine were walking south along the road that circled the island. Ernestine had bundled herself into her poncho and was also carrying the ever-present red umbrella. "You never know when you might need one, especially in spring," she said.

She explained the riddle as they walked.

"The breakthrough came when Edith came across

71

one of Uncle's birdwatching journals. I did tell you Uncle Samuel was a devoted birdwatcher, didn't I?"

Molly hid a grin. Only about ten times! "I think so," she answered.

"Well, Edith, in particular, was Uncle's most frequent companion on his birding expeditions when he first moved here. You see, Edith was recovering from a broken heart—that dreadful Richard Rivington had just jilted her—and she needed distraction. So Uncle had us all out here for a month. He would force her to get up at dawn every day and tramp all over the island with him looking for birds and taking notes. By noon she'd be so exhausted she couldn't even remember who Richard Rivington was."

"Uh—the riddle?" Molly prompted gently.

"Oh, yes, the riddle. Turn right here, dear." Pointing with her umbrella, Ernestine steered Molly into an overgrown lane. "Well, Edith was flipping through this old journal, and she came across a description of a great blue heron. First, there was Uncle Samuel's description, very precise and scientific: 'black crest and markings, back feathers shading from gray-blue to gray' and so forth. And in the margin was one of Edith's mournful little rhymes—she was so miserable, poor dear—about how the heron stalked his prey in a storm-colored coat, a dealer of death who cared not a groat. Or something like that."

"I get it!" Molly was thrilled. "The thing that stalks on stilts and has a storm-colored coat is a heron. The scissors are its beak, I guess. Wow, that's neat! Your uncle made the riddle out of Edith's own poem. *That's* why he said that only you would understand his clues."

"Wasn't he clever?" Ernestine said proudly. "And he truly was a good man. I know Ethel doesn't approve, but I think it's *wonderful* that Uncle was Sammy Slick. I just wish he'd told us long ago."

They left the lane and plunged down a steep, wooded hillside, slithering through muddy undergrowth among leafless trees. "Where are we going?" Molly asked.

"To DeKater Hollow," Ernestine replied. "It's the only place I know of on Blackberry Island where herons live."

The trees thinned out. Through the branches, water gleamed golden in the afternoon sun. Ernestine pointed. "There it is. DeKater Lake."

A twig snapped somewhere behind them. Molly turned, frowning. "Did you hear that?" she asked.

Ernestine shrugged. "There are deer in the woods. Or it could have been a falling branch."

Molly scanned the woods. The trees rose up in a dark mass. She could see no movement among the ranked trunks. Yet suddenly she felt a stab of uneasiness, as if they were being watched. "Let's hurry," she said. "The sun is going to set soon."

They pushed on through a tangle of bracken, and then they were out in the open. "The lake is fed by a little stream on the far side, where those tall reeds are," Ernestine told Molly. "They say the water's quite deep in places."

It was a beautiful place. Still water glimmered before them, a mirror for the willows that dotted its banks. Reeds poked up from the water's surface. Gazing across the shining expanse, Molly saw a tall, slim, blue-gray shape standing motionless by a clump of marsh grass.

"Look," she said in a hushed voice. "There's a heron."

Ernestine nodded. "It's early in the breeding season," she whispered. "They'll just be starting to return from their winter homes in the south."

"So what do we do next?" Molly asked.

Ernestine cleared her throat. "I'm not sure. I mean, this is the herons' home, if we understood Uncle's riddle correctly. Do you think we should search the whole area?"

Molly considered. "That seems like an awful lot of work," she said after a moment. "This is a big place. We could search forever unless we narrow it down some more. Do herons make nests?"

"Yes, they do," Ernestine said, brightening. "Usually in trees that grow on open ground."

"Great!" Molly said happily. "That narrows it down a lot." She gazed around. "There's a big butternut over there. Let's check it out."

The great tree stood by itself near the water's edge. It had four vast, knotty arms, each almost a whole tree itself. As they approached the tree, Molly saw that it was half dead, with dry wood showing through the bark in two of its arms. High and snug in the branches of one of the dead arms was a large, straggling collection of twigs.

She stared. "Is that a nest?" she asked.

Ernestine squinted up at the shapeless bundle. "Yes," she said. "It doesn't look as if it's been occupied for the past few years."

Molly's pulse began to hammer with excitement. "Give me a leg up," she directed. "This could be the place!"

After Ernestine boosted her up, it was easy for Molly to find hand- and footholds on the spreading branches and gnarled trunk of the old tree. She clambered swiftly up to a branch that was level with the nest. Then, inching out along the bough, she peered cautiously into the nest.

It was definitely old. Close up, there were holes where you could see through the nest to the ground below. In one spot, ivy had grown right through the twigs like a green carpet.

"Do you see anything?" Ernestine called.

"I don't think so," Molly said. She wished she knew what she was looking for. A chest of jewels? A suitcase full of hundred-dollar bills?

At any rate, as far as she could tell there was nothing up here at all. Frowning, Molly wriggled back to a comfortable sitting spot and gazed around her. Where else might Sammy Slick have hidden his fortune?

Her eyes narrowed when they fell upon a deep hole a few feet farther up the dead trunk. High off the ground, safe from prying eyes, it was the perfect hiding place.

Molly quickly climbed up to the hole. "Be careful," Ernestine fretted. "The rotten wood might break."

Molly didn't answer. Her head was deep inside the great hole, and she was peering down the hollow trunk. Slanting sun came in through smaller holes in the wood and glinted on metal.

Molly caught her breath. There was something down there!

"Hey!" she yelled. Her voice bounced off the inside of the hollow trunk. Hastily withdrawing her head, she repeated. "Hey! I found something!"

"What is it?" Ernestine clasped her hands in an ecstasy of excitement. "Oh, what is it?"

"It looks like another strongbox. Hand me your umbrella," Molly said as an idea struck her.

Ernestine looked puzzled, but she handed up her red umbrella. Holding it by its tip, Molly lowered the handle down the hole. Down, down . . . her arm was inside the dead tree nearly to the shoulder before the umbrella scraped bottom. She really hoped there were no big spiders living inside the dead bough.

Her face screwed up in concentration, Molly moved the umbrella back and forth, probing with the curved handle. She felt it slide slickly over metal. And then it caught on something.

"I think I've got it!" Molly cried.

Cautiously she hauled up the umbrella, the metal case dangling from the handle.

Hundred-dollar bills danced in front of her eyes.

As the case came into reach, she seized it by its handle and unhooked it from the umbrella. She tossed the umbrella down to Ernestine. Then, tucking the box under her arm, she fairly flew down the tree.

"Here," she said, handing it to the older woman.

"My umbrella came in handy, eh?" Ernestine said. They grinned excitedly at each other.

"Do you have the skeleton key?" Molly asked.

Ernestine delved into her poncho and held up the big brass key. "Right here."

"Try it!" Molly urged.

Ernestine fitted the key into the lock on the box. She gave Molly a quick, exhilarated look, then turned the key. The lid sprang open.

"Oh, no!" Molly and Ernestine cried together. Except for a single folded piece of paper, the box was empty.

"No money," Molly said.

"No jewels, either," gasped Ernestine. "Do you think someone got here before us?"

Molly picked up the piece of paper and unfolded it. On it were four lines of writing.

"I don't think so," she said. "Look, it's another coded message."

The color returned to Ernestine's face. "Thank goodness!" Suddenly she laughed. "Dear Uncle Samuel—he's going to give us a run for our money, I suppose. What does it say?"

"I don't have the code key with me," Molly said. "We'll have to decode it at home."

"Speaking of home, we'd better be going," Ernestine said, peering at the setting sun. "Or your mother will be very angry with me."

She picked up the empty strongbox. "Cheer up, Molly," she added. "All this means is that our adventure is going to last a little longer."

They headed into the darkening woods. As she thought about what Ernestine had said, Molly broke into a smile. "You're right," she said. "I never thought of it that way. Hey, Ernestine, you know what? You're fun. . . . Ernestine?" she repeated when there was no answer.

"Mmmmph!" Ernestine said.

"What?" Molly turned around. Her breath caught in her throat. "*Ernestine!*"

"Mmmmph!" Ernestine said again. It was all she

could say, because her mouth was covered by a large, black-gloved hand. She was struggling frantically in the grasp of a huge, dark figure with no face!

CHAPTER EIGHT

"Help!" Molly yelled. "Somebody help!"

Even as the words left her mouth, she knew no one would hear them. They weren't near any houses or even any roads. The only person who could help Ernestine was Molly herself.

Yelling at the top of her lungs, Molly launched herself at the dark figure. "Get off! Let her go!" she screeched. Kicking and pounding with her fists, she startled the attacker so that he fell back with a muffled cry.

It was only for a moment, but that was enough time for Ernestine to seize her dropped umbrella. Immediately she darted forward and began whacking the assailant on the head with it. "Ruffian! Bully!" she exclaimed breathlessly. "Take that!"

"Aaagh!" the figure in black exclaimed. He flung up his gloved hands, trying to shield himself both from Ernestine's umbrella and from Molly's well-aimed kicks. A moment later he abandoned the effort. Snatching the strongbox from the ground where it had fallen, he fled, crashing away through the woods.

"The box!" Molly cried, starting after him. She was still in a white heat of panic and anger. "He stole our box!"

"Molly, stop!" Ernestine called. "Let him go. It's all right. We couldn't have caught him," she pointed out when Molly turned back to her. "And anyway, there's nothing in the box." She smiled. "I've got the message and the skeleton key safe and sound in my poncho pocket."

"Oh! Good." Molly put her hands on her knees, trying to catch her breath. She looked up at Ernestine. "Are you okay?"

"Oh, yes." Ernestine patted ineffectually at her gray hair, which stood out in spikes all over her head. "Bit of a twinge in my shoulder, that's all. Arthritis." She held up her umbrella. "That's twice today this came in handy. What did I tell you? You never know when you might need an umbrella."

Molly laughed. And then, as reaction set in, her knees buckled and she sat down abruptly on a soft, damp carpet of dead leaves.

"So we were being followed," she said after a

moment. "I thought I felt eyes on us."

"And I thought it was just a deer," Ernestine said ruefully. She pursed her lips. "I suppose we ought to go to the police and report this."

Molly got to her feet. "Yeah, I guess," she said slowly. "Come on, we better get out of the woods before it gets completely dark."

"I tried to pull off that brute's ski mask, but I missed. Could you see who he was?" Ernestine asked as they set off.

That was the question troubling Molly. "No, I couldn't," she said, a frown creasing her forehead. "But there are two other people who know about Sammy Slick."

"There are?" Ernestine sounded startled.

A bit shame-faced, Molly told her about the visit she and Gwen had paid to the Uptons that afternoon. "But we didn't say anything to them about the money," she finished. "And I don't see how they could have found out on their own."

"Nor do I. But we must remember that there's another possibility," Ernestine said. "Uncle Samuel's former colleagues. The ones he said he didn't trust, in his first message."

Molly was puzzled. "But it's been twenty years since your uncle hid the money. Why would they suddenly start looking for it now? How would they know to follow us?"

"I don't know. But remember, they do have one

advantage over us," Ernestine pointed out. "They know who my sisters and I are, though we have no idea who *they* are. If they wanted to keep an eye on us, they could do it and we'd never know."

Molly shivered. "That's creepy."

"Well, we can stop worrying about it soon," Ernestine said. "The police will take the whole matter out of our hands."

"Yeah." Molly's frown deepened.

They walked on in silence for a while. They had just come out onto the main road when Molly sneaked a glance at Ernestine. In the twilight, all she could see was a beaky, irregular profile.

"Ernestine?" she said.

"Yes?"

"What if the police think we're crazy? I mean, who ever heard of a masked mugger in the woods on Blackberry Island? And the story about Sammy Slick's money is even stranger."

Ernestine shrugged. "It's all true."

"But it *sounds* nutty," Molly argued. "And besides, we have no idea who attacked us. The police won't catch him. If we tell them, all that will happen is that the whole world will hear about Sammy's money."

Ernestine frowned. "And so?"

"So maybe we *shouldn't* tell the police. All it will do is mess up our own search."

"Molly, I don't want to stop looking any more

than you do." Ernestine looked anxiously at her. "But, dear child, this adventure is proving to be dangerous. And I could never forgive myself if anything happened to you or your sister."

"Nothing will happen," Molly insisted. "We'll be on our guard from now on. Besides, I gave that guy a few good hard kicks in the shins. So now we know to watch out for a man who limps."

Ernestine smiled, but still looked worried. They were almost at the driveway to Welcome Inn. Molly crossed her fingers. Would Ernestine turn aside, or would she insist on going into town?

After a moment Ernestine sighed. "It is against my better judgment," she murmured. "And Ethel will be furious when she hears. But . . ."

"All right!" Molly whooped.

They went up the long driveway and into the house. Heading into the parlor, Ernestine lowered herself stiffly onto the love seat. "Ooh—ouch, that smarts!" She rubbed her shoulder. "Yes, all right, we'll continue to pursue this adventure in our own way," she said. Leaning back, she closed her eyes and added firmly, "In the morning."

"I am shocked. Shocked, Ernestine," Ethel declared. "How could you be so irresponsible?"

"It seemed right at the time," Ernestine protested feebly, clutching a hot water bottle to her arthritic shoulder.

It was Monday morning, just after breakfast. It was another uncommonly fine, warm day, and Molly, Gwen, and the Biddles were sitting out on the porch. Molly and Ernestine had just finished telling the others about their adventure of the evening before.

"I say you did right," Edith told Ernestine. "Anyway, whoever attacked you and Molly has now had a whole night to create an alibi. It's too late to squeal to the heat."

"Must you use that ridiculous gangster slang?" Ethel complained.

Edith made a show of flicking lint off her pink dress, then aimed a haughty look at the air somewhere above Ethel's head. "Did someone speak, or was that simply the wind?"

Gwen looked at Molly and shook her head.

Molly sighed. Clearly, Edith and Ethel hadn't resolved their quarrel. Edith wasn't speaking to Ethel, and Ethel had been extra-snappish all morning. And it was time to get to work!

She held up the code key she and Gwen had worked out for the first message. "Look," she said. "The important thing now is to decode Sammy Slick's next message and see where it leads us. We have to work fast. We know someone else is after the money, and we *don't* know how much they know."

"Right!" Looking relieved at the change of subject, Ernestine handed Molly the piece of paper with the second message on it. "Decipher away."

Molly settled her notebook in her lap and started writing, her lower lip caught between her teeth as she worked. But after only a moment, she saw that something was wrong. Frowning, she stared at the page she was trying to decode.

The first line of the coded message looked like this: H MDQHTN HJ D, H QLBUN HKO H QHGN.

After Molly used the key to decode the first four words, she had this: k pgskud km g.

"That isn't English," Gwen said, reading over her sister's shoulder.

"No kidding," Molly retorted. She drummed her fingers on the arm of the glider. "Sammy must have used a different code."

Gwen groaned. "You mean we're going to have to go through all that figuring-out stuff again?"

"It's worse," Molly said glumly. "If we stick with the theory that the most-used letter is *E*, that means *N* equals *E*. But if *N* equals *E*, then Edith, Ethel, and Ernestine's names aren't in this message. There's only one word that starts with *E*, and it's the wrong length. We have no easily recognizable words to help us." She slumped back against the cushioned seat, discouraged. The useless code key slipped out of her fingers and fluttered to the porch floor.

"Huh?" Gwen said.

"Dear me," Ernestine said. Picking up the code key, she gazed at it. "Oh! How odd."

"What?" Molly asked without much interest.

"Well." Ernestine pointed to the key. "It's the first four letters of this code key. *S* is *A*, *W* is *B*, *A* is *C*, and *N* is *D*."

"So?" Ethel said, frowning.

"The key letters spell *swan*," Ernestine said. "It's an odd coincidence, that's all."

Molly sat up so suddenly that the glider rocked. "Wait. That's no coincidence!"

"What do you mean, dear?" Ernestine asked.

"It's how the code works!" Molly exclaimed. "Some codes use a key word. You substitute the letters of the word for the first however-many letters of the alphabet, then fill in the rest. For example, with the key word *swan*, your key alphabet would go *S, W, A, N, B, C, D, E, F,* and so on. It sounds simple, but if you don't know the key word, it's really tough to break the code."

"Gracious!" Ethel said. She looked surprised. "You do know the oddest things, child."

"I read a lot," Molly said modestly.

"Do you think the second message is coded the same way?" Ernestine asked. "With a key word?"

Molly nodded. "But I don't know what it is. It's probably another bird, but there are a zillion different kinds of birds."

"There were swans in the graveyard," Gwen said suddenly. "Remember? On the pond."

"That's just what I was thinking," said Edith.

"Right where we found the first message."

Molly stared open-mouthed at her sister. After a second, she said, "I take back everything I said yesterday, Gwen. You *are* good at this!"

Gwen beamed. Edith cast a venomous glance at Ethel. "At least *some* people know how to give credit where it's due," she murmured.

"Swans were where Sammy hid the first message, and herons were where he hid the second," Molly said to Ernestine. "What do you want to bet the key word for the second message is *heron*?"

"I never bet," Ernestine said primly. Then she broke into a big smile. "Oh, isn't this fun!"

After that, it took them only a few minutes to decipher Sammy's second message. When it was done, Molly read it aloud:

A pirate am I, a rogue and a rake.
What others have earned, without mercy I take.
Sweeping down from the north, I rove o'er the main.
But find me at home and I'll lead you to gain.

"That must be a skua," Ernestine said immediately. "They're the pirates of the skies."

"What's a skua?" Molly asked.

"It's like a gull, but bigger and bolder," Ernestine said. "And it's usually brown."

Molly jumped up. "Where do they nest?"

Edith frowned. "Skuas don't often nest this far south," she said.

"I don't know if they're skuas or not," Gwen said, "but there's always a bunch of big brown gulls hanging out by the cliffs near Rocky Point."

"Gwen, you're on a roll," Molly said admiringly. "Let's check it out."

The front door opened and Mrs. O'Brien came out onto the porch. "Molly, Gwen, maybe you're taking up too much of the Biddles' time," she suggested. "They're here to relax."

"They *are* relaxing," Gwen protested.

Ernestine looked startled. "Oh, goodness, the children aren't bothering us in the least!" she said. "We enjoy their company."

Mrs. O'Brien smiled. "Nice of you to say so. Right now, though, I need the girls to run some errands."

"But, Mom—" Molly began.

"Molly . . ." Mrs. O'Brien said firmly.

Molly burned with the injustice of it, but there was nothing she could do. When her mother used that particular tone of voice, there was no point in arguing with her.

When Mrs. O'Brien had returned inside, Molly looked resignedly at the Biddle sisters. "We'll probably be busy for a while," she said. "How about if we meet you at the cliffs at one-thirty?"

* * *

At twenty after one, Molly and Gwen stopped their bikes in front of the pharmacy on Main Street. It was their last errand. They had just come from Grandpa Lloyd's house, where they had retrieved a plastic bag of bluefish he had caught that morning. Molly had picked up the bag the wrong way, and fishy-smelling water had dribbled all over her shirt.

"I'll go in and get Dad's prescription," Gwen offered, climbing off her bike. "You stay here and air out." She wrinkled her nose and disappeared into the store.

"Funny," Molly muttered. Planting her feet on the pavement, she sat back on her bike and looked around, using one hand to shade her eyes.

Suddenly she sat up. Across the street, in Founder's Green—wasn't that Edith? Though she was facing away from Molly, her silver hair and pink dress were hard to miss. But who was the man with her? The white widow's peak of his hair was so dramatic that Molly could see it from all the way across the street.

Just then Gwen came out. "Hey, there's Edith. Edith! Miss Biddle! Hi!" she called, waving so hard she nearly dropped the bag she was holding.

To their surprise, instead of waving, Edith took the strange man's arm and started walking away. "I guess she didn't see us," Gwen said.

"She's going to be late for our meeting at Rocky

Point." Molly commented.

Gwen suddenly grabbed her sister's arm. "That man Edith's with. He has a cane. He's limping!"

Molly saw what Gwen was driving at. "Gwen," she pointed out, "look at his white hair. That guy must be seventy. He couldn't have followed me and Ernestine through the woods and jumped us. He's probably got arthritis or something. That's why he's limping."

"Oh." Gwen let go of Molly's arm. "Yeah, I guess you're right. Sorry."

"You're such a maroon," Molly said, grinning. "Come on, now *we're* going to be late, too."

Five minutes later, pumping their pedals madly, they raced up to Ernestine and Ethel, who were waiting at the cliff by Rocky Point.

"Sorry we kept you waiting," Molly puffed. "We saw Edith in town. Isn't she coming?"

Ethel sniffed. "I suppose that headache she pleaded was an excuse to avoid my company," she said. "Edith is so childish sometimes."

"Well, let's not worry about Edith right now," said Ernestine. She pointed to the big brown birds that swirled around the cliff. "They *are* skuas. You're such an observant girl, Gwen!"

"Thanks," Gwen said, glowing.

"The trouble is, how are we going to get up there to look?" Ethel asked. "I certainly can't clamber about on cliffs with my arthritis. And neither can you, Ernestine, so don't say you can."

"Yes, I can," Ernestine said stubbornly.

"No, you can't," Molly told her. "Especially after you hurt your shoulder yesterday. Sorry, but Ethel's right." She handed Ernestine the smelly packet of bluefish. "You guard the fish. Let Gwen and me do the climbing."

Ernestine's face fell. "Oh, all right," she grumbled. "Be careful." She unhooked her red umbrella from her arm. "Here. You might need this to poke around in the cracks."

Molly and Gwen moved to the cliff. It was really little more than a steep jumbled slope of boulders, easy enough to scramble up if you used your hands as well as your feet. The skuas' nests were along a broad, sandy ledge near the top.

"One word of caution," Ethel said.

Molly turned around. Over Ethel's shoulder she could see the condo construction site at Rocky Point. Antlike figures in hard hats were lifting beams and girders into place.

"Skuas don't like intruders in their nesting areas, particularly if they're brooding," Ethel said. "It's quite early in the season, so I doubt there'll be any eggs yet. But watch your step all the same. They can be aggressive."

"Okay," Gwen said, looking doubtful.

Together, the two girls scrambled up the rocks. Molly held the umbrella under her arm.

"Krraaa! Krraaa!" They were just about at the ledge when harsh squawking erupted above them. Molly and Gwen looked up. A big, brown skua wheeled in the sky over their heads, glaring down at them. Then another. And another. Soon the air was full of them.

"Uh-oh," said Gwen.

In the next instant, the birds were diving toward them like so many screaming brown bombs.

"Take cover!" Molly yelled, shielding her head with her arms.

CHAPTER NINE

An instant later the birds had engulfed Molly and Gwen in a brown, swirling cloud. Beady eyes and vicious, curved beaks flashed past Molly's face. Close up, the sound of their wings was like thunder, and their harsh cries were like foghorns. Through the noise, Molly could hear Gwen's frightened cries.

Then Ernestine's voice joined the din. "The umbrella, Molly!" she called. "Use the umbrella!"

The umbrella? For a second, Molly couldn't comprehend what Ernestine meant. Then she got it.

Balancing precariously on a boulder, she unsnapped the band around Ernestine's umbrella and opened it. *Whoosh!* A giant flower of red cloth expanded over her head. The startled skuas fluttered backward, squawking louder than ever.

"Gwen, get over here!" Molly shouted. "Come under the umbrella with me!"

Gwen didn't need to be told. She was already scrambling over the rocks to take shelter.

In seconds the skuas recovered from their fright and began to dive at Molly and Gwen once more. Molly closed the umbrella and then shot it open again. *Whoosh!* Once again the big birds backpedaled in the air.

"Keep opening and closing the umbrella, Molly!" Gwen panted. "It scares them."

Molly nodded grimly. "Are you okay?"

"I think so," Gwen replied.

"Children!" Ethel called. "Come down right away. It's too dangerous. Come down, I say!"

"We're not quitting now!" Gwen yelled back. Molly glanced at Gwen in surprise. She was pale, but to Molly's surprise she wasn't in a panic. "I'm okay," she said. "But let's hurry up and find Sammy Slick's third clue, or whatever it is, so we can get out of here."

At first, Molly kept the skuas at bay with the umbrella while Gwen poked into the deep crevices between the rocks with a stick she found. After a few minutes, Molly's arms got tired and they switched tasks. All the while, the angry screaming of the birds rang in their ears.

"I don't know how much longer we can keep this up," Gwen said when she handed the umbrella back to Molly. "I never knew opening and closing an umbrella could take so much out of a person!"

Molly nodded. "I'm beat, too. If we don't find whatever Sammy left here in the next five minutes, I think we'll have to give up for now." Gazing at the wheeling cloud of birds, she added, "Maybe it's time for Plan B. If only I *had* one!"

"Forget about Plan B!" Gwen suddenly called in a muffled, but triumphant, voice. "I just found a strongbox!"

Molly took her eyes off the skuas and looked around for Gwen. It took her a moment to spot her. Gwen's whole upper half had disappeared into a deep chink between two giant boulders. A moment later she emerged, clutching a tarnished metal box in both hands.

"All right!" Molly cheered. Relief and excitement gave her new strength, and she pumped the umbrella vigorously. "Good job, Gwen! Now let's get out of here."

Leaping like mountain goats from boulder to boulder, the two girls raced down the slope. They tumbled to a halt in front of a horrified Ethel and Ernestine.

"Oh, gracious! Are you all right?" Ernestine cried, grabbing each of the girls by the hand.

"We're fine," Molly tried to tell her.

But now Ethel was lamenting. "I'm to blame. I should never have permitted this reckless expedition," she said. "Never!"

"But look," Gwen said, holding out the strongbox. "We found it!"

Molly glanced up at the skuas. Now that the intruders were gone from their nesting area, the birds' frenzy was leaving them. Dozens of them still roiled and shrieked in the sky, but at a safe distance.

"Here," she said, handing Ernestine's umbrella back to her. "You know, I'm beginning to think I should carry one of those myself."

"After we went to all that trouble, all we got was another poem—" Gwen grumbled.

"Written in mirror letters just to make our lives a little harder," Molly chimed in. They'd had to hold the original note up to a mirror and copy the letters, which had all been written backward.

"And now we can't even crack the stupid code," Gwen complained. Scowling, she tore yet another page out of her notebook, crumpled it up, and tossed it into the Biddles' fireplace.

"I can't figure out what we're doing wrong," Molly muttered. They had tried *skua* as a key word, but after they ended up with "rzq waiz hpmlwvoozd rz lvqcz dafl py psd" as a first line, they knew they were on the wrong track. Next they'd tried *heron* and *swan*, but neither of those worked, either.

Molly glared at the coded note. "This is really, really frustrating!"

It was Monday evening. The Biddle sisters were downstairs in the dining room, having their first taste of Mr. O'Brien's cooking. Judging by how long they seemed to be lingering down there, Molly thought, they must be enjoying it.

Thanks to David O'Brien's growing fame as a chef, the inn's dining room was often filled these days, and the O'Briens had recently hired a part-time waiter. Andrew, Molly and Gwen's brother, earned a little money as the busboy and dishwasher. The new arrangement left Molly and Gwen free during the evenings. Usually Molly liked it that way, but tonight she felt as if she'd almost prefer helping Andrew with the dishes.

"Well," she said, rubbing her eyes, "we're not getting anywhere. I say we give up the decoding for now. Maybe it'll make more sense in the morning."

"Okay," Gwen agreed with obvious relief.

Molly tossed the coded note into its box on the coffee table. Then she reached into the wooden crate full of Samuel Biddle's mementos and pulled out the stack of photos. "Why would Sammy Slick make a puzzle so hard no one could solve it?" she wondered aloud. "He doesn't *look* mean."

"Want to hear something strange?" Gwen said as Molly glanced through the photos. "You remember that man we saw with Edith in Founder's Green this afternoon? When I asked her who he was, she said she didn't know what I was talking about. She said she didn't meet any man in Founder's Green."

"But we both saw them together. Why would she lie?" Molly asked, puzzled.

"Maybe it wasn't her after all," Gwen suggested. "We only saw her from the back."

Molly didn't answer. She was staring down at the New Year's Eve photo of Sammy Slick with the younger members of his gang. She felt as if her heart had stopped beating.

"What's wrong?" Gwen asked. "You're breathing funny."

"Gwen," Molly croaked, "look." She pointed to the laughing, dark-haired young man immediately behind Sammy Slick. Though his face was mostly in shadow, there was just enough light on it for Molly to make out his dramatic widow's peak.

"It's the guy who was with Edith," she whispered. "He's one of Sammy's gang!"

"Oh, boy," Gwen said. "We better warn Edith!"

Molly stared ahead with a troubled face. "Unless she already knows," she said slowly. "It would explain why she lied about being with him."

Gwen's blue eyes grew round as she understood what Molly was saying. "Oh, *boy!*" she repeated.

Shaking her head, Molly stood up. "I don't know what's going on," she said. "But we better find the sisters and talk this whole thing over."

They hurried downstairs with the photo. The dining room was still full, but the Biddle sisters weren't there. Molly and Gwen found Ethel and Ernestine in the parlor, having coffee. "Edith's in the library looking for something to read," Ernestine explained.

It was just as well Edith wasn't there, Molly thought. She held out the photo and pointed at the man with the widow's peak. "Do either of you know who this is?" she asked.

Ethel took the photo from Molly and squinted at it. Then she reached into her cardigan pocket and fished out her glasses. "Can't see a blessed thing without them," she grumbled. Perching them on her nose, she bent over the photo again.

When she raised her head, her face was blank with surprise. "Why, good gracious," she said in a shocked voice. "Why didn't I see it before? That's Edith's old beau, Richard Rivington!"

Everyone in the room froze for a moment, staring at Ethel. Then Ernestine swiped at the old photograph. "Let me see that!" she said.

Her face darkened as she gazed. "It *is* him," she breathed. "And with another woman, behind Edith's back! I always knew he was a rat."

"Ernestine, that isn't the point! Besides, this picture was taken in 1945, and Edith didn't meet Richard Rivington until 1946," Ethel reminded her sister.

"Let me get this straight," Molly said. Her thoughts were churning. "Richard Rivington was really a gangster?"

"It appears so, though we certainly had no idea," Ethel said. "Thank goodness he ran off before Edith could persuade him to marry her."

"Thank goodness he's out of her life!" Ernestine added.

Gwen and Molly looked at each other.

"Uh, well, that's the problem," Gwen said.

"What do you mean?" Ethel looked impatient.

"We mean he *isn't* out of her life," Molly said. "We saw them together today, in town."

"Impossible!" Ethel declared.

"He vanished fifty years ago," Ernestine objected.

"He's long gone," Ethel agreed.

"Besides, she'd never speak to him again after the way he jilted her," Ernestine added. "What woman would?" Then she broke off, a doubtful expression on her face.

"Actually, Edith might," Ethel said after a minute.

Ernestine nodded ruefully. "Knowing Edith, in fact, it's very likely."

"It's *true*," Molly said urgently. "She did take him back. We saw them. And later Edith lied about it." She glanced from Ethel to Ernestine. "You see what that means, don't you?"

An awful silence fell. In the middle of it, the parlor door opened. "Hello, everyone," Edith said brightly. "Am I missing the fun?"

* * *

"I believe Edith," Gwen said. "I don't think she knew Rivington was a member of Sammy's gang."

Molly pondered, her chin on her fist. "I do, too," she said at length. "Even though I can't understand how she can still like him. He sounds like such a creep."

"And he looks like Count Dracula," Gwen put in. "That hair!"

It was ten o'clock that night. Molly and Gwen were in Molly's room, eating cookies they'd smuggled up from the kitchen and talking over what had happened earlier that evening.

When Ethel had first accused Edith of deceiving them, Edith had admitted it. "Yes, it's true, Richard came back to me three months ago," she said haughtily. "And, no, I didn't tell either of you. Why should I? You would only have badgered me and tried to turn me against him. But that's because you don't understand him. You don't understand what true love is."

Ethel snorted. "What rubbish!"

"But, Edith dear, how could you take him back after the way he treated you?" Ernestine asked.

Edith tossed her head. "Oh, Richard explained all that. It's a long story, but he had family troubles. His father died in disgrace and he had to take care of his mother and sisters. He felt he couldn't ask me to be his wife under such circumstances. I think it was very noble of him."

"You believed that?" Gwen burst out. "I'm only nine, and I don't believe it."

"Gwen!" Molly scowled at her sister.

And so it had gone on for a while. But when Ernestine showed Edith the photo of Rivington with Sammy Slick, there was no mistaking Edith's bewilderment and dismay. "He couldn't be a gangster," she kept saying. "There must be some mistake. He couldn't be!"

"You think perhaps he found himself at the wrong New Year's Eve party by accident?" Ethel said acidly. "There's no mistake, Edith. Look at the picture, and read the caption. Richard was one of Sammy Slick's men."

It was time to find out some important facts, Molly thought. "How much did you tell Mr. Rivington about Sammy Slick's money?" she asked Edith. "Does he know everything?"

Edith looked down at her lap. "Yes," she admitted. "Of course I've been telling him everything. He's my fiancé, after all."

"But you swore not to tell *anyone*!" Gwen said, shocked.

"Edith, we don't want to hurt you," Ernestine said sadly. "Do believe us. But don't you see what Richard is up to? Don't you see why he came back to you after all these years? Don't you see why he's here on Blackberry Island now? He's after Uncle's money, and he's using you to get it."

"That isn't true," Edith cried. "Richard came back to me because he loves me! He didn't even know about the money until I told him, and he's only here because I asked him to come."

"Poppycock," Ethel pronounced.

Edith's plump face crumpled and she burst into tears. That was when Ernestine looked at Molly and Gwen and said, "Girls, I think you'd better leave us alone with her."

Now, in Molly's room, Gwen sighed. "Poor Edith. How can you get to be as old as she is and still do such dumb things?"

Molly uncrossed her legs and leaned back against the wall, staring absently across the room. "Gwen," she said. "Let's stop talking about Edith for a second."

"Okay," Gwen agreed. "What do you want to talk about?"

"Rivington," Molly said promptly. "He knows everything we know—the codes, everything. I'm worried that if we don't work fast, he's going to find the money before us."

Gwen looked up at Molly from under her eyebrows. "I have a feeling I'm not going to like what you're about to say," she remarked.

Molly nodded. "Sorry. But we have to try to crack that last code again. Now. We can't waste any more time."

"But you know it's past my bedtime," Gwen argued half-heartedly.

"It's vacation, remember?" Molly said. "Mom and Dad will let us stay up late."

"Okay," Gwen grumbled. She climbed off Molly's bed. "Let's go down and get the message from the Biddle sisters." She aimed a finger at Molly. "But *you* get to knock on their door."

The two girls headed down to the second floor. When Molly knocked on the Biddle sisters' door, Ernestine stuck her gray head out.

"Shh. Edith's just cried herself to sleep," she whispered. "What's wrong, girls?"

"Nothing," Molly whispered back. "We just wanted to borrow the third message from you. We're going to work on it some more."

"The third message?" Ernestine stared at them. "But don't you have it already?"

Molly felt a sudden stab of alarm. "No. We left it in the strongbox, on your table," she said.

"Oh, dear," Ernestine said faintly. "Dear me. Are you sure?"

When Molly nodded, Ernestine stepped back and held the door open. Molly and Gwen peered in and saw that the coffee table had nothing on it. Molly felt a chill.

"When we came back to our room, the box and the skeleton key were gone. We assumed you had them in your room." Ernestine explained. "We also thought you were the ones who left the window open."

Molly pushed past Ernestine and hurried to the window. There was a tiny smear of mud on the sill.

"Oh, no!" she gasped. It was suddenly, horribly clear what had happened.

The Biddles' suite had been burgled. And Sammy Slick's message had been stolen!

CHAPTER TEN

"Uncle's message, in the hands of the enemy!" Ernestine groaned. "This is terrible!"

Ethel came to the door beside her sister. "Keep your voice down. What on earth are you talking about?" she asked irritably.

Ernestine explained about the missing box.

"What? That's impossible," Ethel said. "How could anyone steal the box right out of our room?"

"Sammy Slick's gang specialized in cat burglary," Molly said. She felt like crying. "Remember?"

Ethel shook her head. "He must have climbed one of the porch pillars, right out in front of the house, while we were in the parlor."

Gwen looked accusingly at Molly. "I told you he

was the bad guy, but you wouldn't listen to me. Remember how he was limping? I said maybe he was the guy who attacked you in the woods, but you said he was too old."

"Well, it seemed impossible," Molly protested feebly.

"He wasn't too old to climb up and break into our second floor, was he?" Gwen retorted.

Molly stared miserably at her feet. Gwen was right. If only she had listened!

"I wonder how he did it," Ethel said. "If his arthritis is anything like mine, it must have been tough going."

Ernestine wasn't paying any attention. "Think of all the people in the dining room who might have seen him!" she said. "I must say, I am shocked that even that rat Rivington could be so brazen. But I suppose one shouldn't put anything past that scoundrel." She scowled. "Look what he did to Edith."

"We better get my parents," Molly said.

"No," Ethel declared. When Molly looked at her in surprise, she added, "I don't want them to feel responsible for this. It wouldn't have happened if we weren't here, engaged in this rather dubious quest. It's our problem."

"At least there's one thing going for us," Gwen said.

"What?" Molly asked glumly.

"We never decoded the message," Gwen pointed out. "Maybe Rivington won't be able to do it, either."

"Keep your fingers crossed," Ernestine said. "That's our only hope."

And on that note, gloomy and worried, everyone went to bed.

During the night a strong wind sprang up and swept in cold, bracing air. It must also have swept some cobwebs out of Molly's brain, for she woke up the next morning with the obvious solution to their problem.

Leaping out of bed, she ran downstairs and dashed into Gwen's room. "Get up!" she called.

"What's wrong?" Gwen sat straight up in bed, wild-eyed and with her dark hair in tangles. "Is there a fire?"

Molly laughed. "No, you loon. There's no fire. I just thought of something. Remember all those scratch pages we threw in the fireplace when we were trying to figure out the code yesterday? We copied the whole message onto scrap paper, remember? Because it was in mirror writing. So we can use our notes to reconstruct the message."

Squinting, Gwen rubbed sleep out of her eyes. "You mean—"

"Yes!" Molly said. "I mean we still have a chance to find the money! Let's go tell the Biddles."

Gwen climbed out of bed. "Well, okay," she said, then yawned widely. "But don't you think you should get dressed first?"

"Oh." Molly looked down at her flannel nightgown. "I forgot about that. Be back in a minute."

She ran back up to her room, pulled on some jeans and a T-shirt, and dragged a brush though her hair. Then she hurried into the bathroom, splashed water on her face, and brushed her teeth. "Ready," she muttered, and ran downstairs again.

When they knocked, a subdued, red-eyed Edith let them in. "I hope you children don't think too badly of me," she said. "I suppose there's no fool like an old fool. At first I couldn't believe Richard would have deceived me. But after I heard all the facts . . ." She trailed off, dabbing a white lace handkerchief to her eyes.

Molly felt both sorry and embarrassed. "Well, it could have happened to anyone," she murmured.

"The thing I can't understand is why he would steal Uncle's message," Edith said. "It seems so pointless! I was telling him everything I knew about the search." She sniffled. "Well, I suppose it's just his nature. Once a thief, always a thief, as Uncle used to say."

Molly was relieved when Ethel and Ernestine came in from the other room. Quickly she explained her idea about reconstructing the coded message.

To her surprise, Ernestine remained glum. It was

Ethel who nodded briskly and said, "Good! Let's try it."

Ernestine sat down in one of the chairs by the fireplace. "Is there any point?" she asked with a sigh. "Richard Rivington has had more than twelve hours already to crack the code. He's probably already found the money."

"Snap out of it, Ernestine!" Ethel ordered. "Don't tell me you've lost your sense of adventure just when I've found mine." To Molly and Gwen, she added, "Her arthritis must be troubling her. Changes in the weather always make it worse, you know. But she'll come out of her funk, don't worry. Now, girls, let's have a look at those scraps of paper."

Grinning, Molly retrieved the crumpled pages she and Gwen had tossed into the fireplace. She spread them out on the coffee table. "I think we might be able to find the whole message on here. We worked on all different parts of the message, trying to decipher it."

"It's a good thing we didn't light a fire this morning," Ethel said. "Edith wanted to."

"I still do," Edith said, clutching a woolly white sweater around her. "It's chilly today."

"Look, there's the first line," Molly said excitedly. "I recognize all the Z's."

Ethel squinted at the wrinkled piece of paper, which bore the letters PZO WSFZ ENJIWVMMZA

111

PZ IVOUZ ASCI NY NQA. "Gracious, what a jumble," she said, looking somewhat taken aback.

Soon Molly and Gwen had pieced together the rest of the lines. "We should call this the Z code," Gwen said, surveying the reconstructed message. "Look at all those Z's!"

Ethel looked thoughtful. "When you solved the first code, you said that you started by assuming that the most-used letter had to be *E*," she told Molly. "Shouldn't we assume Z stands for *E*?"

"I guess so," Molly agreed. "But it doesn't get us very far. *E*'s only one letter."

"It's a start," Ethel said firmly. She wrote down Z = E. "We now know that Z is the fifth letter of our key alphabet."

Molly frowned. She'd noticed that when you used a key-word code, Z usually didn't change its position (unless it was a letter of the key word), because it was the last letter of the alphabet. Did that mean the key word of this code had a Z in it? Or was it not a key-word code after all?

An idea was tickling the back of her mind. Something about mirror-writing . . .

Suddenly she let out a yell. "I've got it! It's backward! Like the mirror-writing!"

"What?" Gwen said.

Molly grabbed a pencil and a fresh sheet of paper and started scribbling furiously. She was testing her theory.

A few seconds later she gave a cry of satisfaction and showed the page to Ethel and Gwen. PZO WSFZ had turned into "men have."

"In this code, the alphabet runs backward," she explained. "After the key word, *skua*, the first letter is Z, then Y, then X, and so on."

"I get it," Gwen said. "So Sammy wrote the message in mirror-writing as a clue."

"Right." Molly handed blank pieces of paper to Gwen, Ethel, and Edith. "We'll each figure out one line. We'll be done in no time!"

Ten minutes later the poem was ready. Molly handed it to Ernestine, who had shed her gloomy mood as if by magic. "Will you read it to us?"

Ernestine smiled and took the paper. Holding it up, she read:

Men have worshiped me since days of old.
I burn, but my heart's glow I do not spend.
I glitter as though I am made of gold.
Find me and find your journey's end.

"Goodness, how romantic," Edith said, with a quaver of emotion in her voice.

"'Find me and find your journey's end,'" Gwen quoted. "Do you think that means we'll finally find the money?"

"Yes, I think so. But what does the rest of it mean?" Ethel asked.

"You mean you don't get it?" Molly asked with a sinking heart.

Ethel shook her head. "It rings a bell, but . . ."

"So many bird species have been worshiped by various peoples throughout the ages," Edith said. "For example, ancient Egyptians held the ibis sacred. And then, of course, there's the eagle—"

"Oh, do be quiet and let us think," Ethel interrupted. "We must be going about this the wrong way."

"Well!" Edith looked wounded.

They sat in silence as the minutes ticked away. Molly was afire with restlessness. She tried to concentrate on the meaning of the riddle, but her thoughts kept wandering to Richard Rivington. Had he cracked the code yet? Had he solved the riddle? Was he at this moment looking at Sammy Slick's money and rubbing his hands with glee?

What *had* made him rob the Biddles' room? she wondered. He must somehow have found out that they were on to him. But how could he have known?

Maybe he'd been lurking outside the parlor for some reason when they were confronting Edith, Molly thought with a shiver. It was scary to think of Rivington hiding in the shadows, watching without anyone knowing he was there. But, then, that was what being a cat burglar was all about.

As if reading her mind, Edith said, "Richard, a

cat burglar! I still can't believe it." She heaved a sad sigh. "I'll never look at my sweet little kitty cat the same way again."

Kitty cat. Kitty cat. The words rang in Molly's ears like an incantation. She caught her breath. "Kitty the cat," she said aloud.

"I beg your pardon?" Edith said politely.

"Kitty the cat," Molly repeated. She'd just had a crazy idea. . . .

"What's the name Kitty short for?" she asked excitedly.

"Kathryn, usually," Ernestine said. "Why?"

"Is there a name that starts with *T* that you could make into Kitty?" Molly persisted.

"None that I can think of. What is this about, Molly?" Ernestine asked.

"Kitty Upton. Her first initial is *T*. I remember thinking it was strange when I saw it in the phone book. So why is she called Kitty?"

"Perhaps the *T* was her husband's initial," Edith suggested.

Molly shook her head. "Her son's name is Donald Junior, so her husband must have been Donald, too."

"Good heavens, what does it matter?" Ethel wanted to know.

"It might matter a lot," Molly said. She took a deep breath. "Don't you think Kitty is a perfect nickname for a lady cat burglar?"

CHAPTER ELEVEN

Everyone stared at Molly. Then Edith said, "Are you saying you think Kitty Upton might be the one who robbed us? Not Richard?"

"I know it sounds crazy," Molly answered. "But I think it might be right."

"But, good heavens, whatever makes you think it isn't that rat Rivington?" Ernestine sounded exasperated. "We *know* he was in Uncle Samuel's gang. We *know* he lied to Edith. And why else would he turn up again after all these years?"

"I don't know why," Molly said. "But, like Edith said, he turned up *before* any of you knew there was any money to be found. If you didn't know, how could he have known? And also, the rest of it doesn't really make sense. Okay, maybe he found out somehow that we knew who he was, and that's why he burgled the suite last night. But why attack me and Ernestine in the woods yesterday? Why risk it, when he knew that Edith would tell him everything she knew?"

"Well, those are good questions. And there's also the *how*," Ethel admitted. "How did he manage all those athletic feats? As I said, I certainly couldn't have managed to climb up to a second-story window with *my* arthritis."

"Oh, my," Edith breathed, her wrinkled face radiant with hope. "Is he really innocent?"

Molly jumped up and walked to the fireplace. She couldn't believe she was talking this way to the ladies, especially when she was so unsure of her own reasoning.

"I don't know," she said at last. "I just think it's possible."

"But why pick on Kitty Upton?" Ethel asked. Impatience was creeping back into her voice. "I mean, a nickname is well and good, but it isn't much to go on, is it?"

Molly bit her lip. There wasn't one big reason—just a lot of small ones that were starting to add up. Like the attack on Ernestine and herself coming right after their visit to the Uptons. Like the third message being stolen after they'd found it at Rocky Point, where Donald Upton worked.

"She was a weird lady," Gwen said unexpectedly. "She gave me the creeps, the way she was so interested in Sammy Slick. And she said mean things about you guys. Especially Edith."

"That's right," Molly nodded, remembering. "She was going on about how Edith stole other people's boyfriends."

"I never did!" Edith said indignantly. "I never loved any man but Richard!"

"And we didn't even meet Kitty Upton until Uncle moved here," Ernestine put in. "Edith certainly didn't flirt with any men then. She was still too upset about Richard."

"You didn't meet Kitty Upton until then," Molly said slowly. "But maybe *she* knew *you* before. If she was in Sammy's gang, she'd have known all about his dear nieces." Kneeling by the box from the attic, she rummaged through the photos and pulled out the one of the New Year's party again. Holding it up, she pointed to the fair-haired woman whose arm was around Rivington's shoulders. "And if one of them stole her boyfriend, Richard Rivington, she'd be pretty mad, wouldn't she?"

Edith gasped. "But I had no idea!"

"Just a minute," Ethel said, holding up one hand. "Interesting as this line of thought is, we must remember that it is only speculation. We can't see that woman's face. We don't know who she is. In fact, we have not a shred of proof that Kitty Upton was in Uncle's gang."

"Oh, I *know* it's true," Edith said, clasping her hands. "I know Molly is right, and Richard is innocent."

"Whether he's our thief or not, that man is not innocent," Ernestine said sharply.

"Ernestine's right," Molly agreed. "I didn't say he was innocent. I just think he might not be the one trying to beat us to Sammy Slick's fortune, that's all."

"Wherever it is," Ernestine added.

Gwen sighed. "All this what-iffing is making my brain hurt," she said plaintively. "What if the code starts with *Z* instead of *A*? What if the bad guy is really someone other than we thought? I wish we could talk about something we actually *knew* for a change."

"The child is right," Ethel declared. "We all need a break. What does everyone say to a nice brisk walk?"

"Oh, lovely," Ernestine agreed.

Molly shrugged. "Okay," she said reluctantly. She didn't really want to take a break, but she had to admit that she felt the same way as Gwen. Her brain *was* starting to hurt.

"Brr! You go ahead. I'm staying right here where it's warm," Edith said with a shiver.

So, collecting sweaters and jackets, Ethel, Ernestine, Gwen, and Molly left the house.

They crossed the lawn and made their way down a twisting wooden stairway to the rocky, deserted beach. Wind whipped at Molly's long hair, sending it sliding in a dark curtain across her face. Pushing it out of her eyes, she looked back.

Above them, Welcome Inn's jumbled collection of peaked roofs and chimneys rose starkly against the sky. Molly loved that view. From the beach, it appeared that the old inn was the only building for miles around, standing alone against the wind and the sea.

"Come along, Molly," Ethel called.

Molly turned around. Already, the Biddle sisters were a good distance down the beach, striding out powerfully. Gwen, behind them, was half trotting to keep up. Molly ran after them.

"I thought old people were supposed to walk slowly," Gwen panted when Molly caught up.

Ethel glanced over her shoulder. "I heard that. For your information, a brisk walk every day keeps one feeling young and vigorous," she said.

"But I still *am* young and vigorous," Gwen complained. "So can't I take it easy?" She put up a hand to shield her face. "Besides, the wind is blowing sand in my eyes."

Ernestine smiled. "Isn't it wonderful? So wild and lonely. When I was your age, a day like this would have inspired me to great adventures. I know! A game will take our minds off our problems.

Why don't we pretend we're in the Sahara desert, caught in a sandstorm?"

A game? Molly and Gwen exchanged glances. "Does she think we're babies?" Gwen whispered.

But Ernestine was off and running. "Yes, that's it," she said enthusiastically. "We're a tribe of roving Bedouin. Who wants to be the sheik?"

Neither Molly nor Gwen spoke up. "Oh, come now," Ernestine reproved. "Surely one of you wants to be the sheik?"

"Ernestine, I don't think you have any takers," Ethel said.

Ernestine waved a hand. "Nonsense. Why, the sheik is the ruler of all Arabia! He's got riches galore! Pearls of great price, and blood-red rubies, and frankincense and myrrh in sandalwood boxes—"

She broke off, staring at Ethel. So were Molly and Gwen. For Ethel had stopped walking in mid-stride and clapped a hand to her forehead. "Oh, good heavens, of *course*!" she cried.

"Of course what?" Ernestine sounded peevish.

"Of course, that's what Uncle's riddle must mean," Ethel said.

"What? What?" Molly, Gwen, and Ernestine all yelled at once.

"The firebird, from the *Arabian Nights*. The bird that burns and then rises again from its own ashes," Ethel said. "The fabulous phoenix of antiquity."

Molly's eyes shone. "The phoenix," she repeated

softly. Now it all made sense. Of course!

"But the phoenix is a mythical bird. It doesn't really exist. Gracious, how are we ever going to find a phoenix's nest?" Ernestine lamented.

"Maybe we needn't find its nest. This riddle doesn't end with 'find me at home,' the way the others do," Ethel said. "It just says 'find me.'"

"'Find me and find your journey's end,'" Gwen quoted again. "I liked that line."

"You guys," Molly said. "Don't you see? 'Your journey's end'—it doesn't just mean the end of the search. It also means home. You'll find the phoenix at home."

Ernstine gasped. "You mean—"

"Yes. The andirons!" Molly said. "And those fireplace utensils you've been carrying around all these years. They're shaped like phoenixes."

"Wow! It sounds like *The Maltese Falcon*," Gwen said. "We rented that movie last week."

Molly nodded. "That's why Sammy Slick had the andirons made. Remember, Gwen, Kitty Upton told us the fireplace in Sammy's room didn't work at the time. She couldn't understand why he had all those fire utensils made. Well, I bet you anything *that's* where he hid the money."

Everyone stood there for a second. Then Ethel threw back her head and laughed aloud. "What are we standing here for?" she asked. "We may be seventy-one years old, but I'll bet you children can't beat Ernestine and me back to the inn!"

Laughing, the four of them set off toward Welcome Inn. In their excitement, none of them looked back. But even if they had, they might not have spotted the black-clad figure that was following them at a discreet distance.

"Oh, hello," Edith said when they crowded into the suite. Looking pleased with herself, she gestured at the fireplace, where an untidy heap of logs lay across the andirons. "I was just about to light the fire."

Everyone stared in horror.

"Don't!" Ethel commanded, striding forward.

Edith's hand, poised to strike the match, froze. "But why ever not? It's a perfectly good fire, even though I had to lay it myself because the house is absolutely deserted—"

"We know where Uncle's money is!" Ernestine said.

"Oh!" Edith raised a fluttering hand to her chest. "Oh, where? Where?"

"Right here," Molly said. With reverent hands she picked up the heavy phoenix-headed poker. "Inside these birds."

"Go on, smash it," Ernestine urged.

Gwen came up beside Molly and peered at the phoenix with its painted red and purple feathers and its glowing green eyes. "It's so pretty! It's a shame we have to break it," she said.

"I know. Well, let's do it," Molly said. Her heart pounding, she gripped the poker by its pronged end and swung the heavy head against the stone of the fireplace.

Thunk! With a dull thud, the poker rebounded off the stone. Vibrations ran down the metal shaft and shook Molly's entire body.

"It didn't break," Ernestine said in disappointment. "Here, let me try."

"Wait!" Molly said. Something had caught her eye. She held up the phoenix. "Look at this."

Where the bird had struck the stone, it was flattened. A gleam of bright yellow shone through where the red and purple paint had scraped off.

Everyone crowded around, staring at the poker. "Why," Ernestine breathed. "Why, it's—"

"Solid gold!" Gwen and Edith cried together.

"Gold!" Molly whispered. Goose bumps broke out on her flesh. She had a fortune in her hands!

"Let me see," Ethel demanded. She took the poker from Molly, then patted her pockets with her free hand. "Where are my specs, drat them?" she muttered. "Must have left them in the bedroom."

Bearing the poker with her, she disappeared into the other room. Meanwhile, Ernestine had picked up the phoenix-headed shovel and was scraping at the paint.

"It's gold, too," she confirmed, awe in her voice.

"I guess they all are."

"Oh, this is wonderful!" Edith caroled. "We're rich, rich, rich!"

A small sound came from the doorway of the suite. Flushed with joy, Molly turned around.

Suddenly the blood felt frozen in her veins. For standing in the doorway was a tall figure, dressed in black with a ski mask covering his face. And in his hand was a gun.

CHAPTER TWELVE

In another second everyone else had spotted the intruder, too. The words Ernestine had been about to utter died on her lips. Gwen let out a small, frightened whimper. Molly clutched her sister's hand and squeezed it hard.

Edith's face turned chalky. "Richard?" she said in a strained whisper. "Is—is that you?"

The figure in black made no reply. Instead he advanced into the room, circling around toward the fireplace and beckoning with his free hand for Ernestine to hand him the shovel. He moved with a slight limp, Molly noticed. But the hand pointing the gun at them never wavered.

"You won't get away with this," she said, trying to keep the quiver out of her voice.

"That's right," Ernestine chimed in. "Robbery in broad daylight! The police will catch you in no time. You might as well—"

As the gun moved toward her she fell abruptly silent.

The man in black was now standing to the left of the fireplace, having herded Molly, Gwen, and the two old ladies into the corner of the room. He reached down to pick up one of the andirons.

Whump! Suddenly there was a dull thud. The gun clattered onto the hearthstones as, with a muted groan, the man crumpled to the floor.

Behind him, Ethel was revealed in the bedroom doorway, the phoenix-headed poker in her hand still raised to strike. "There! That ought to hold him for a while," she said breathlessly.

For a split second, everyone stared at her in utter confusion. Then Molly let out a joyful yell.

"Ethel! You saved the day!" Bounding forward, she threw her arms around the old woman and kissed her wrinkled cheek. "You're the greatest!"

Gwen pointed to the hearth. "Look," she said. "The gun broke!"

It was true, Molly saw. The weapon had split neatly in half. "It's just a plastic toy," she gasped. "It isn't a real gun at all!"

Then everyone was talking at once. Ethel was explaining how she'd heard the sudden silence while she was in the bedroom and, looking through the open door, had seen the man with the gun. Ernestine, her face wreathed in smiles, kept saying, "Well done! Well done!"

It was Molly who noticed that Edith wasn't joining in the mirth. Her face still dead white, she was staring as if hypnotized at the man who lay on the floor.

"Who is he?" she asked tensely. "I must know. But I'm afraid to look."

"Oh, you poor dear," Ernestine said gently. "Here, we'll find out together."

As the man stirred and moaned, Ernestine bent down and addressed him. "My sister is standing over you with a poker," she informed him, "so I'd advise you not to try anything. Now take off that silly ski mask."

The man slowly reached up. Molly looked anxiously at Edith, who was clasping her hands so tightly that the knuckles were white.

Then, with a sudden, defiant movement, the man tore off the black wool mask. Molly found herself staring into the pale, furious eyes of Donald Upton, Jr.

"Here's Sheriff Choate," Gwen announced, leading a wiry, gray-haired man into the room.

After Ethel had called the sheriff, Molly and Ernestine had tied their prisoner's hands and feet with the tasseled curtain ties from the drapes.

Through it all, Donald Upton had shouted and raged. "I demand to see my lawyer!" he yelled.

"Oh, shut up!" Ethel snapped.

Now the sheriff gazed at the bound figure lying on the sofa and blinked. "Looks like you're in a bit of a jam, Don," he remarked.

"Sheriff, these women assaulted me! That one over there in black struck me with a blunt instrument!" Donald Upton raved.

When the sheriff looked inquiringly at her, Ethel shrugged. "It's true," she admitted. "But he was threatening my sisters and those two dear children with a gun. How was I to know it was only a plastic toy? And after he attacked Ernestine in the woods the other day, I certainly had reason to believe he was dangerous, didn't I?"

The sheriff was looking confused. "I think we better start from the beginning and tell him the whole story," Molly said.

"Good idea," agreed Sheriff Choate.

And so the whole story came out, with Molly and Ernestine doing most of the talking—although Gwen kept interrupting to brag about all the good ideas she'd had. As the tale unfolded, Donald Upton seemed to shrink into himself on the couch.

Finally Molly stopped talking. The sheriff looked at Donald Upton.

"Well, Don, it's a pretty wild tale. Your mother a cat burglar! My goodness!" He shook his head. "But

I must say the facts seem to bear these folks out. You got anything to say for yourself?"

Donald Upton scowled. "It was all Mother's idea," he muttered. "I didn't want anything to do with the whole nutty scheme. But she had this bee in her bonnet ever since the old days when she was part of Sammy Slick's gang."

"We were right about Kitty Upton!" Molly whispered to Ernestine.

The sheriff had produced a small notepad and pencil and was scribbling away. "Go on," he said to Donald Upton.

"Mother was always convinced Sammy Slick had squirreled away a fortune somewhere," Upton said. His mouth tightened, and for a moment Molly was struck by how much he looked like his mother. "And she was right, wasn't she? All Slick's holier-than-thou talk about stealing from the rich and giving to the poor was just a load of hogwash. He was keeping his share the whole time."

"Uncle said all the money he left us was gained by legitimate means. And if Uncle said that, you can be sure it's true," Edith said stoutly.

Donald Upton looked at her and snorted. "Right, lady. And if you believe that, then I've got a bridge to sell you."

"Why, you rat!" Ernestine said hotly. "Uncle was an honorable man!"

The sheriff cleared his throat. "If we could get

back to the subject?" he murmured.

"Excuse me," Ernestine said, flushing.

"And so when Molly and Gwen here came around asking questions about Sammy Slick, your curiosity was roused, is that it?" the sheriff asked Upton.

Upton nodded sulkily. "Mother overheard them in the yard talking about a strongbox, and she figured they were on to Slick's hidden loot. So she put me up to following them. I guess you know the rest already."

"I guess we do," the sheriff agreed. "Well, Don, looks like you and your mother are going to be guests in my jail tonight." He looked worried. "Though where exactly we'll put you I don't know. That room was turned into our extra file room years ago."

A sudden idea hit Molly just as the sheriff was herding his prisoner out the front door. "Sheriff Choate," she piped up. "If Mr. Upton's in jail, what will happen to the Rocky Point condo development?"

The sheriff scratched his chin. "Good question. Don is the developer. I don't guess all his contractors will want to go on working for him while he's behind bars. They'd never be too sure of getting paid, you see. No, I suspect that the Rocky Point development is going to be put on hold for quite some time, young lady."

"Excellent!" Molly felt a grin stretching across her face. *That* news was going to make it a whole lot easier to tell her mother about everything else that had happened since the Biddle sisters came to town!

"He's coming, he's coming!" Edith drew in a fluttering breath. "Oh, how do I look? Is my hair all right?"

"You look beautiful," Gwen told her.

It was true. Learning that her beloved Richard Rivington wasn't the one trying to cheat them out of Sammy Slick's money had made a new woman of the youngest Biddle sister. Even her silver hair seemed to glow with happiness.

That afternoon Ernestine, Ethel, and Edith had gone into town; the older sisters to take the precious fireplace set to a bank for safekeeping, and Edith for a private talk with Richard Rivington. Even though he hadn't been after her money, he still had a lot of explaining to do.

Judging by the glow in her eyes when she came back, his explanations had been good enough for her. But she refused to say what he'd told her. "I invited him to the inn for tea," she said. "Let him tell you himself."

"That rat?" Ernestine exclaimed. Then, catching Ethel's stern eye, she subsided. "I suppose we ought to hear him out," she admitted.

While the ladies were gone, Molly's parents had

come home, and Molly had steeled herself to tell them about the incredible adventure. She was worried that they might hold the Biddle sisters responsible for putting her and Gwen in danger.

The interview had gone reasonably well, she felt, though she suspected her parents weren't fully satisfied with the rather vague account she'd given of the more dangerous bits.

"But how on earth could you have known all along it was just a toy gun?" her mother had asked.

"Oh, Mom, don't you know anything? It was obvious, that's all," Molly said, trying to sound confident.

After a while her mother had sighed in resignation. "Well, I suppose we can't hold the Biddle sisters responsible for you girls," she'd muttered. "Goodness knows *we* can't ever stop you from doing exactly as you please."

Now it was five o'clock Tuesday evening. Richard Rivington was coming up the driveway in Blackberry Island's one taxi. Molly grinned with happy anticipation. Imagine when Josh Goldberg heard that she'd had tea with an ex-gangster!

"I think I'll meet him on the porch," Edith said, and rushed out of the parlor. A few moments later she reappeared, beaming and leading a handsome elderly man with a cane and an impressive white widow's peak.

Catching sight of Edith's sisters, he bowed from

the waist. "Ethel, Ernestine; you're looking well," he said.

"Richard," Ernestine murmured stiffly.

Turning to Molly and Gwen, he took each of their hands and shook them solemnly. "I've heard a lot about you ladies," he said.

"We've heard a lot about you, too," Gwen said, staring frankly at him. "Ernestine says you're a r—"

"Really interesting person," Molly jumped in quickly.

Ernestine made a noise in her throat. "I'm sure you know that's not exactly what I said, Richard."

"Yes," Ethel chimed in. "You'll have to do some pretty fancy explaining if you want Ernestine and me to accept you as our sister's beau."

Rivington looked apprehensive.

Edith sat down on the love seat and picked up the teapot. "He can explain over tea," she said firmly. "Everyone sit down, and I'll pour."

Molly had a sudden sense of *déjà vu* as she perched on one of the chairs and took a cucumber sandwich. Was it really only three days ago that the old ladies had arrived with their suitcases full of gold? Was it really only three days ago that she and Gwen had sat here with them, drinking tea and wishing Mrs. O'Brien would come to their rescue? She smiled. It felt now as if she'd known the Biddles for years.

Richard Rivington sipped his tea, then cleared

his throat. "I suppose I ought to start from the beginning," he said, "when Kitty Upton and I first joined Sammy Slick's gang."

"Yes, do," Edith said. "Tell them why you became a—what was it? A second-story man?"

"Yes. I had a brother, Ted, who was ten years older than me. Ted was one of the original members of the gang. I worshiped him, and I was full of ideals about helping the poor. So naturally I wanted nothing more than to be in Sammy's gang myself. After Ted was killed in World War Two, Sammy let me have my chance."

"Strange choice for a role model," Ethel muttered, but Molly saw that her expression was a bit less severe.

"Kitty Pound—that was her maiden name— came on the scene at about the same time," Rivington went on. "She was the daughter of Sammy's best friend and partner, Jim Pound. Before her father died, he had trained her until she was just about the best cat burglar around.

"Kitty was trouble from the beginning, though. To start with, she soon grew tired of Sammy giving away all the money to poor people. She thought he was foolish and sentimental. She didn't see why we shouldn't keep it ourselves. And later she became convinced that Sammy was really keeping most of the money for his own enrichment while we all stayed poor."

Molly thought of the angry woman raging about how Samuel Biddle had wasted money. Yes, that made sense.

"But that's not all," Edith said eagerly. "Tell them what she did to you, Richard!"

Richard Rivington looked embarrassed. "Well, I'm afraid it makes me seem rather a cad," he said. "But Kitty and I—well, we were rather an item for a while. Until I met Edith, that is." He took Edith's hand and pressed it tenderly.

"What happened then?" Gwen asked, wide-eyed.

"Well, once I met Edith I knew there was no other woman for me," Rivington explained. "Of course, I knew Sammy wouldn't approve—he had terribly torn feelings about being a gangster at all, and the notion of his nieces ever getting involved with that world upset him very much. He wouldn't have wanted me to marry Edith, but I thought we could bring him around, once he saw how much in love we were."

"Go on," Ernestine said.

"The trouble was, Kitty never gave me the chance to square things, either with Sammy or with Edith," Rivington said sadly. "When I told her that we were through, she was furious. She went straight to Sammy and told him I'd been toying with Edith's affections."

Rivington sighed. "And that was the end.

Sammy was very angry. He made me swear to leave town immediately and never to contact Edith again. He said she'd never be happy with me if she knew what I truly was, and that it was better to hurt her by leaving without explaining than to hurt her by staying and dragging her down." He shrugged helplessly. "I did as he said. I kept my promise to him for fifty years—until three months ago, when I was in Chicago and I saw Edith by chance at the supermarket." He and Edith stared soulfully into each other's eyes. "When I saw her then, as lovely as ever, I knew I couldn't let her go a second time."

Gwen sniffled. "Wow," she said, taking a bite of an eclair. "What a romantic story!"

"Sentimental nonsense. You're a couple of saps," Ethel murmured, then blew her nose with a honk.

"Richard, I'm sorry I thought ill of you," Ernestine said sincerely. "You're a good man."

Molly had a lump in her own throat. Usually mushy stories just made her uncomfortable, but for some reason this one didn't.

"Mr. Rivington, how did the gang break up?" she asked.

"Well, I did keep in touch with one or two of the old gang members, even after I left," Rivington answered. "Apparently Sammy dissolved the gang a few years after the war ended. The economy was booming, people were prosperous, and he felt that our work was no longer quite as necessary as it had been. And since he'd always felt so torn about what he did anyway, I suppose he just seized the opportunity to call it quits."

Ernestine smiled. "I remember how happy Uncle was when he retired. All he ever really wanted to do was putter around and study birds."

"And what about Kitty Upton?" Molly asked.

"Yes, how did that awful woman end up running Upton House?" Edith chimed in.

"I can only guess," Rivington replied. "As I told you, she grew more and more suspicious of Sammy, believing that he had kept a secret horde of money from our work so that he could live the rest of his life in luxury."

"Well, in a way she was right," Ethel pointed out.

"I imagine Kitty and her husband bought Upton House so that she could keep an eye on Sammy," Rivington said thoughtfully. "She probably hoped that if she waited long enough, eventually she'd discover where he was hiding the loot, and then she could grab it for herself."

"She almost did," Molly said with a shiver. "It took her fifty years, but she almost succeeded."

"Yeah, but she never would have done it if we hadn't cracked all the codes," Gwen boasted. "Specifically me."

Everyone laughed.

Just then Mr. O'Brien stuck his head into the

room. "Molly, phone for you," he said. "It's Josh."

Surprised, Molly hurried to the kitchen. "I thought you weren't coming back till tomorrow," she said into the phone.

"Hey, O'Brien, don't say hello or anything," Josh said.

"Hello. I thought you weren't coming back till tomorrow," she repeated.

Josh sighed. "The skiing was a bust. It rained since Sunday, so we left early. So—what's been going on at home? I bet things have been pretty quiet, huh?"

Why did he sound so certain of himself? Molly wondered, nettled.

Gwen came into the kitchen and tugged at her sleeve. "Hold on," Molly said.

"Did you tell Josh how I cracked the code?" Gwen asked anxiously. "Did you tell him about the man with the gun? Did you tell him about the gold?"

"Not yet," Molly whispered. Grinning, she turned back to the phone. "Well, it *has* been pretty quiet," she said to Josh. "But I do have a couple of little things to tell you. . . ."

WELCOME INN

Here's a sneak preview of Welcome Inn #4:

The Spell of the Black Stone

It wasn't till the whole family was sitting in the front parlor later that night that Molly remembered the package from Uncle Jack. Hurrying out to the hall table, she grabbed it and brought it back into the parlor.

"Pennyahael," her father pronounced when she showed him the strange postmark. "It's a town on the Isle of Mull, in Scotland. Jack's there visiting one of his old professors."

Molly unwrapped the brown paper eagerly. Inside were two books. *Celtic Legends* was the title of the one on top. The other was called *Myths and Folktales from the Scottish Islands*.

"Books? Is that all?" Gwen's voice was disappointed.

Though she didn't say anything, Molly was disappointed, too. She loved to read, and she liked myths and legends a lot, but usually Uncle Jack's presents were a little more—well, unusual.

When she tossed the brown wrapper into the metal trash can, it clanged. "Hey, stupid, there's something else in there," Andrew said.

Molly pulled the wrapper back out of the can and shook it. A smooth, black stone fell into her hand, and a sheet of notepaper fluttered to the floor.

"It's a note from Uncle Jack," said Gwen, picking it up and handing it to Molly.

"Dear Molly," she read. "Scotland seems alive with magic. Being here is like being in one of the books I've sent you. They'll tell you all about the kinds of magical creatures, or Sith (pronounced *shee*), that you might encounter here. And the stone, I'm told, will give you mastery over one of them. It's called a Sith-stone, and the man who sold it to me assures me that it's genuine. However, I did notice he had dozens of identical ones in a drawer in his shop. I suspect he does quite well selling them to gullible tourists like myself. Oh, well, the carving is interesting. If nothing else, it'll make a nice paperweight. Happy birthday. Love, Uncle Jack."

Intrigued, Molly studied the black stone. It fit perfectly into the palm of her hand. An intricately carved pattern of twining serpents decorated its surface.

Opening *Celtic Legends*, she stopped to stare at the frontispiece. It was a painting of a magnificent black horse in the act of plunging into a turbulent river. On the horse's back was a young woman in flowing clothing, her mouth open in a scream. "The Kelpie carries Janet Beaton to a watery grave," said the caption. "Kelpies can take the form of beast or man."

"Cool," Molly said aloud. She flipped through the book, looking for more pictures.

There was one of a mermaid seated on a rock, calmly combing her long tresses while in the background a man struggled to keep from drowning. "The treacherous mermaid ignores the sailor's cries for help. Mermaids lure men to their deaths by singing," said that caption.

"Creepy," murmured Gwen, who was looking over Molly's shoulder.

Molly shot her an annoyed glance and moved to the loveseat. Curling her feet under her, she opened to the beginning of the book and began to read about the Selkie, whatever that was. As she read, she rubbed her thumb absently over the back of the Sith-stone. It had a funny texture, so smooth and friction-less that it felt wet, though Molly knew it wasn't.

Outside, the wind's shrieking climbed to a higher pitch. Mrs. O'Brien got up and moved to the window. "This storm is really something," she said, sounding worried.

FZZT! A bolt of lightning temporarily made the parlor as bright as day. At the same instant, thunder cracked right overhead.

A split second later, the lights went out and the room was plunged into darkness.

WELCOME INN

Secret in the Moonlight
0-8167-3427-5 $2.95

Ghost of a Chance
0-8167-3428-3 $2.95

The Skeleton Key
0-8167-3429-1 $2.95

The Spell of the Black Stone
0-8167-3579-4 $2.95
Coming in January 1995

Available wherever you buy books.